The Tho
That Counts

J. J. Overell

illustrations by Robin Lawrie

Acorn Editions
Cambridge

for my parents

Acorn Editions
P.O. Box 60
Cambridge
CB1 2NT

British Library Cataloguing in Publication Data:
A catalogue record is available from the British Library.

ISBN 0 9065 5416 0

Copyright © J. J. Overell 1997
Illustrations: Copyright © Robin Lawrie 1997
Reprinted 1998 (twice)
Reprinted 1999

Printed in Great Britain by
St Edmundsbury Press Ltd., Bury St Edmunds

Contents

Sunflowers

Sally stood by the window. From the sixth floor flat she looked out over rows and rows of streets. It would never be a cheerful view and the grey, overcast sky didn't help. It was the first of May, but there were no trees or gardens in sight to tell you it was Spring.

Sally had moved so many times she had lost count. Now she and her Mum were here in a new town. The flat wasn't bad, much better than some of the places they'd stayed. But the town was big and strange.

And Sally had changed schools so many times she had lost count of those, too. The teachers tried to be kind, to help her settle in. But each school had its own ways, you couldn't get to know them all before you'd made a fool of yourself. That's what Sally dreaded most – being made to look a fool.

"Sally, dear, what are you doing?"

"Reading, Miss."

"But that's your Home Book. You should have your Class Reader out now."

"What are you doing, Sally?"

"My maths, Sir."

"But you're using your pen, Sally. We never, ever use pen in our maths books, do we class?"

"No, Mr West," the class would chorus.

She imagined rather than heard the other children saying, "Look at Sally Smith, isn't she stupid? She doesn't know anything."

"What are you doing, Sally?"

"Going out to play, Miss."

"But you haven't got your pencil case. It's Tuesday. We always take our pencil cases out on Tuesday, don't we class?"

"Yes, Miss."

And Sally would look around to see that all the other children were leaving the room with pencil cases expertly balanced on their heads.

That last one hadn't really happened. But Sally had come across so many peculiar rules that she would sometimes while away the long playtimes by thinking up some of her own.

But she learnt quickly and had found that the best thing to do was to keep quiet and watch the others. Just keep yourself to yourself and copy the others. She sighed.

Her mother called from the kitchen, "Have you got rid of it yet?"

Sally's Mum had asked her to throw away a tall shrivelled plant that stood on the floor by the window. The last people must have left it. She looked at it again now. It was as tall as her. She didn't know what kind of plant it was. It had a spindly stem and a head which it couldn't hold up, resting against the glass of the window. It was attached low down by green string to a supporting stick which was far too small. The whole plant had dried to a light brown but the leaves hadn't fallen.

"What about the pot?"
"It's cracked. Throw the whole lot."

So she did. And thought no more of it until a few days later, in school. It was still her first week at her new school. Her teacher, Mrs Jaffray, had given Sally a reading book from a scheme she'd never seen before. She was reading a story about sunflowers. There were pictures. She was reminded of the plant in their flat. But it wasn't quite the same. One of the pictures showed two children looking up at a sunflower which was twice as tall as they were. And the plant in the book was healthy and colourful, with lush Jack-and-the-beanstalk leaves and a huge head, held up high, not drooping, fringed with long, yellow, velvety petals, like flames. The whole head was like a sun. A sun. Perhaps that was how they got their name.

"Sally, come and read please."

Sally took up her book and read the rest of the story to Mrs Jaffray who then signed her reading card. Sally was about to go back to her place when Mrs Jaffray asked, "Are you enjoying the book, Sally?"

"Yes, thank you."

"Which story have you liked best so far?"

"This one – about the sunflower." And she found herself telling Mrs Jaffray about the plant in their flat. Mrs Jaffray was interested and asked more questions. But Sally was now aware that the other children were also listening. She answered briefly and was anxious to get back to her place.

The class soon settled back to their reading. Except for one girl. Alison couldn't concentrate on her book any more. She couldn't wait until break time. She had to speak to the new girl, Sally Smith.

"Alison, read your book, dear," Mrs Jaffray looked thoughtful. She didn't often have to tell Alison to get on.

Sally usually spent playtimes alone, watching the other children laughing and playing. She didn't feel left out, she was used to watching from the side. And sometimes, like today, she would stand by the fence, looking through it to the world outside.

"Hello, I'm Alison."

"Yes," Sally replied, still gazing through the fence.

"You're Sally, aren't you?"

"Yes."

"Do you like our school?"

"It's all right."

"Have you just moved here?"

"Yes."

"Where do you live?"

"Bramble Tower."

Alison had been watching Sally closely and now she jumped with excitement.

"Flat 64?"

"Yes," said Sally, turning round at last. "How did you know?"

"I knew it must be!" said Alison. "It was ours!"

"What was?"

"That plant you found *was* a sunflower. It was Jodie's and mine. She used to live there."

"Jodie?"

"She's my best friend. We were always in the same class. She lived at Flat 64, Bramble Tower. I've been there lots of times. But last summer they moved away. Down south." She paused for a moment, before adding, "And now you've moved into their flat."

"But – the flower?"

"We were doing this topic last year on Growth. We had partners. Jodie and I were together, as usual. We all planted sunflower seeds. When they started to grow we had to draw them and measure them. Later on we were allowed to take them home. Jodie was going to look after ours to start with and then we were going to plant it out in my garden.

"Then, during the summer holidays, they had to move. I don't know why." Alison had been talking rapidly, now she continued more slowly, as they started to walk together round the edge of the playground. "The flat must have been empty all that time. And the sunflower got forgotten. We said we'd write to each other, but we never did. I still miss her though. And she's still my best friend. Perhaps I'll write to her now and tell her about the plant," she looked up again and stopped walking. "I bet you miss your friends."

"Yes," said Sally. But as she tried to think about the children at her last school she struggled to picture any of their faces and found that she couldn't recall even one name. As for friends. . . .

"Did you keep any of the seeds?" Alison asked suddenly.

"No."

"That's a pity, we could have tried again."

When Sally got back to Bramble Tower that afternoon she went straight to look in the dustbins on the ground floor. But they had all been emptied. She had been hoping to find the bag she brought down the other day and rescue some of the seeds. She was surprised at how disappointed she felt.

In the flat Mum was getting tea ready. Sally went over to the window. She got down on her hands and knees and moved her hands gently over the carpet. She knew what she was looking for. There had been pictures of the seeds in the book, they were quite big and stripy – black and white. The boy and girl had planted a handful, though only one had grown.

But the carpet was clean, her Mum had hoovered it that day. She ran her fingers along the gap between the carpet and the skirting board, right underneath the window. The carpet was loose. She pulled up the edge, away from the concrete floor. There was a line of dust right against the skirting board and one, two – no – three sunflower seeds. All three were small and grey, rather than stripy. One was thin and papery, but the other two were thicker, Sally felt more hopeful about those.

She made herself be calm and ever so gently picked the seeds out of the dust and went to look for an envelope. She put the seeds inside and sealed it up, putting sticky tape on the places where there was no gum. She was taking no chances. She labelled the envelope in capital letters, "SUNFLOWER SEEDS – HANDLE WITH CARE" and put it in her school bag.

Later, over their meal, she told her Mum all about Alison, Jodie, the plant and the three seeds. Her Mum was pleased. Sally didn't often talk about the other children at school.

"You can ask that Alison round for tea if you like. One day when I'm not working. And if the seeds don't grow, we can always get some more."

"Oh no," Sally said. "It's got to work with the ones I've found. Seeds from a packet wouldn't be the same."

The next morning it was Sally who couldn't wait to speak to Alison. They gloated over the seeds as if they were priceless jewels. Mrs Jaffray gave them a padlock key and they were allowed to go to the school shed and help themselves to whatever they needed. They filled a pot with compost, made three holes with a stick, dropped in the seeds and gently pressed the compost down to cover them.

They watered the pot and kept it in the classroom stock cupboard, checking it several times each day, during breaks.

Mrs Jaffray knew how disappointed they would be if nothing happened, but felt she should prepare them for this possibility. One day she warned them that the seeds might not be fertile.

"What does that mean?" asked Sally when Mrs Jaffray had left the room.

"It means they might not be able to grow at all."

They had to wait eight days. But finally, on one side of the pot a small, doubled-over shoot broke the surface, with a lump of soil, like a little hat, balanced on top of it. Four days later they transferred the seedling to a larger container. They put the first pot back in the cupboard, but the other two seeds never did germinate. Sally wondered which of the three seeds had grown.

Three weeks after it first appeared they took their seedling to Sally's flat, where they placed it on the windowsill. It was now June and the high, south-facing window was ideal for providing plenty of light. Light was what it needed to grow, Alison said. Photosynthesis. That was the proper word. Sally and Alison began to use it all the time.

"Don't forget to water it," nagged Alison. "And whatever you do, don't move down south."

Alison stayed for tea.

11

In another fortnight the plant was 43 centimetres tall, too tall for the stick in the pot. They took it round to Alison's house and dug a hole for it near the wall in the back garden, again, south-facing for the best of the sunshine. Alison's Dad gave them some more compost to put round it.

Sally stayed for tea.

The plant prospered and at last the flower-head began to form. The other children in the class were following its progress, too. "How's the sunflower?" at least one person would ask each day.

"It's photosynthesising beautifully."

"How tall?"

They always knew exactly.

68 centimetres. . . .
One metre and one centimetre. . . .
One point three three. . . .
One metre sixty-seven. . . .

Alison's house was only two minutes from the school, so just before the end of term Mrs Jaffray made arrangements with Alison's Mum and took the whole class to see it. They could just all fit into the garden without treading on the borders. Alison's Mum gave them squash and a biscuit. This time when they measured it, the plant had topped two metres. Everyone cheered.

In September the girls were in Year Six and had a new teacher. But Mrs Jaffray remembered to ask them how the sunflower had done.

It had reached two metres twenty-nine centimetres by the middle of August when the flower opened. By the middle of September the petals had faded and Alison's Dad said it was time to cut down the head. They had had to borrow his step-ladder to reach it and his secateurs to cut through the thick, rough stem.

The seed head was beautiful, a perfect circle, gently domed, more than twenty centimetres across. Most of the surface of the dome was made up of tiny yellow stars. Where these had withered in the centre they were starting to fall away to reveal the grey tops of the fat seeds below. A few petals, still yellowy, clung at the edges of the circle and while they were looking a green and brown beetle climbed out of the spiky green fringe. They put the beetle onto another plant in the garden and left the seed-head in the shed to dry out.

"Why not bring it in for Harvest Festival?" suggested Mrs Jaffray a couple of days before the school service.

So they did. In fact, it became the centre-piece of the Harvest display and got a special mention from Father Tom.

It looked more beautiful than ever and smelt like a florist's shop. It had dried to a light brown and had become much lighter in weight, too. The tops of all the seeds were now visible. They were arranged in long curved lines, making wonderful patterns.

"What shall we do with it?" asked Sally as they were helping to clear away after the service.

"Keep the seeds for next year," said Alison.

"But we won't need them all."

"We could keep some for the birds in the winter."

"Yes. And people in the class might like some."

When they asked, everybody wanted some. Mr Baldwin let them use a maths lesson. First he made them guess how many seeds they thought there would be. Then, Sally and Alison broke into the tight, grey dome. It was hard to winkle out the first seeds, but once started they began to pop out as if they were alive. The other children crowded round the table and scooped them up in handfuls to be taken away and counted. There were more than anyone had expected. After two counts the total was agreed at one thousand six hundred and seventy-six.

Half would be for the birds. That wasn't too difficult – eight hundred and thirty-eight. The other half was to be shared equally between the twenty-nine children.

"Can we use calculators, sir?"

"Certainly not. You can practise your long division."

They groaned.

"Let's divide it by thirty," suggested Alison.

"Why's that?"

"Well, it'll be easier. And I'd like to send some seeds to Jodie. If that's all right with Sally."

Sally went red. She said, "If you like." But everyone could see she was upset.

At break time Alison saw Sally on the far side of the playground, on her own, looking through the wire fence. Sally didn't turn round when Alison walked up and stood beside her. Alison remembered the first time she had spoken to Sally, it had been just like this. "I thought it would be nice to send some seeds to Jodie," she said. "Don't you think? After all, she was my best friend."

14

"Was?"

"Silly Sally," Alison laughed when she'd said it. "Silly Sally, silly Sally." She said it again because it sounded funny. She wasn't being nasty. And Sally laughed with her.

That night Sally told her Mum that she hoped they wouldn't be moving again for a while. Her Mum said she hoped so too.

The Bonfire

"Michael!"

Micky had his Saturday all worked out. He was going to spend it building a bridge across the stream in the woods. This was his latest idea. Micky had lots of ideas. But when he heard his name shouted, he knew that the Bridge Project was going to have to wait.

It was his Dad shouting. Micky knew why his Dad was shouting and because of that he was not surprised that he could hear him, even though he was in the kitchen and his Dad was at the bottom of the garden. He knew his Dad was at the bottom of the garden because he must have just opened the shed door.

Until that moment, until the shout, Micky hadn't thought about the shed and what was in it since last Saturday. He'd been busy with several other Projects since then.

Dad had been putting on his outdoor shoes when Micky came down for breakfast that morning.

"I'm just going out to mow the lawn, Micky," his Dad had said.

"O.K, Dad," he'd replied cheerfully. He hadn't twigged. Only now did Micky remember.

"Dad. . . ." he said quietly, pleadingly, though his Dad couldn't possibly hear him. He would be staring, red-faced, into a wall of cardboard where his normally tidy shed should have been.

"Michael!" Even louder this time.

"Coming, Dad," Micky whined, climbing down from his stool and moving reluctantly towards the back door. That's where he met the red face.

"I'm going out, Micky. I'm going to the Garden Centre. When I get back, in about an hour, my shed is going to be back to normal. Yes?"

"Yes, Dad."

"What's it doing there, anyway?"

"It's for the recycling."

"That was last week."

"We collected it last week, but we needed somewhere to put it. I thought you wouldn't mind if we put it in the shed for a day or two."

"A day or two?"

"Yes, well, I just have to find out who we send it to. . . ."

"Send it to? Send it? What, by post? I thought you had this all worked out. I thought this was part of some scheme. An official scheme."

"No, not exactly. It was an idea I had. You see, I reckoned if we could. . . ."

"Enough! Just get rid of it Micky, before I get back. O.K?"

"Yes, Dad."

Max was half way through reciting his telephone number when Micky interrupted him.

"Max, you've got to help me."

"What is it now?"

"You know that cardboard we collected?"

A pause.

"Yeeess." Max was being cautious.

"We've got to move it."

"You've found somewhere?"

"Not exactly."

"What then?"

"Dad's found it."

"You didn't tell him?"

"I forgot."

"You forgot? How could you forget? We spent all day getting that stuff. How could you just forget?"

"Well he didn't get back till late that night. By the time he got home we were working on the Pond Project, remember?"

"Yes, I remember. Mum says she's never buying me another pair of jeans."

"Max. Pleeease."

"I'm watching Football Fiends."

Micky was desperate. But then he had an idea. "Max!"

"What?"

"We'll have a bonfire."

"I'm on my way."

Micky put down the phone, already regretting what he had just said. He hadn't thought this through. Not even as far as usual. It had been a spur of the moment thing. A bribe. He knew Max would come if he offered fire.

"We told all those people that their cardboard was going to be recycled," said Micky as he watched Max begin to get the cardboard out of the shed. "We said that not only would a waste material be turned into something useful but at the same time we would be preventing the release into the atmosphere of carbon dioxide." Micky paused. He hadn't expected Max to be impressed by his little speech, so he wasn't disappointed.

"They'll never know," said Max, without stopping.

"That's not the point!" Micky was indignant. "They trusted us."

"It's only a bit of cardboard, Micky. What difference does it make? There are factories all over the world belching out carbon dioxide and things far worse all the time anyway."

"If you think like that no one will even try to do anything about pollution," Micky protested.

But Max could not be stopped now. "Besides," he said, "What else could we do with it? A bonfire's the only sensible thing."

"You would say that."

"What do you mean?"

Micky sighed. It did seem the only way. "Come on then, let's get it lit," he said, "it's gone ten already. We've only got half an hour."

"Oh Micky, you're a genius. This is the best idea you've ever had." Max was staggering out of the shed with another armful of cardboard bundles.

They had started the fire in the round, metal bonfire frame. It was already going well and even Micky had forgotten all about recycling. Max's enthusiasm was so convincing. It felt like they really were achieving something worthwhile. What a fire! This wasn't like trying to get rid of damp grass cuttings. This stuff *wanted* to burn.

It was Micky's job to tend the fire in its early stages while Max got more cardboard out of the shed. But only on the understanding that soon they would swap over.

It was becoming clear that there simply wouldn't be enough time to wait until everything in the frame had burnt before putting on more.

"We can put it round the outside as well," Micky suggested.

Max threw down his load and hurried back for the next. "Two more, then it's your turn."

"Wow. It's getting really fierce here." Micky pulled off his sweatshirt and wiped his face with it. "Hey, Max, bring the rake will you? I can hardly get close enough now."

Max used his last load as a shield against the heat before hurling it at the flames. The flattened boxes missed the target, sliding and scattering at the base of the fire, but there was no retrieving them.

"Get the rake, Max. That lot needs shifting."

With his arm up to shield his face, Max retreated into the shed and reappeared with the rake. He managed to push back a couple of boxes but then they noticed how the cardboard on the top of the fire was beginning to lift gently, borne up by the intense heat.

"Give it here," Micky ordered. "Fetch something else. I'll hold the top bits down."

With the rake held at arm's length and twisting his body away, Micky was just able to endure the heat while the end of the rake rested on top of the lifting sheets.

The rake was knocked out of his hand when Max threw another huge armful of boxes on top.

"You idiot!" Micky yelled.

"Don't worry, they're tied up. They'll burn more slowly and keep the others down."

And for a while the flames were contained under the latest, teetering bundles. But beneath them, the growling in the bonfire frame was like a big cat preparing to pounce. And already

the nylon string around the bundles was withering, evaporating.

"Get the rake!" Max shrieked. "The handle will catch light soon."

The rake had fallen so that the teeth were wedged on the top of the frame. Micky didn't notice that, he just lunged for the handle and pulled.

The bonfire frame, the whole inferno, tumbled towards them. The shock of it sent them both reeling. They were on the ground, on all fours, crawling away from the heat. They crawled until they reached the sudden cold of the gap between the shed and the back wall. There they sat, huddled and shivering.

When Micky heard the shed windows shatter and fall in and the substantial crackling of wood burning, he began to cry silently.

Then above the fire, his father's voice, "Micky!"

Later, when he was thinking back, what surprised Micky was how calm his Dad had been.

At first his Dad called for him several times. Micky had never heard him shout so loud. The shouts he had heard from him earlier that morning were nothing in comparison. And though he tried to answer, he found he couldn't. No sound came.

It was Max who replied at last. "Uncle Jim. Uncle Jim! We're here!"

"Max? Is that you? Are you hurt? Are either of you hurt?"

"No. No, we're O.K."

"Stay there. Stay there! Don't move!"

Their narrow space was now becoming unpleasantly warm and they were beginning to feel stifled, but soon they heard the sound of water from a hose playing against the other side of the shed. In a few minutes the roaring and splintering began to die down. It was getting cooler and over the top of the shed they could see that the angry black clouds of smoke were turning a softer grey. Then Micky's Dad came round to get them.

And he had been so calm.

He took them quickly round the smouldering ruins, squelching through puddles in the blackened grass and into the house.

"I was a bit worried about the petrol in the lawnmower," he said. "But the old Shirehorse didn't let us down, the fuel tank held out."

The boys sipped their drinks. They didn't know what to say. Just to say sorry wouldn't be enough.

"Uncle Jim. . . ." Max began.

Micky's Dad interrupted, "Do you know what?" he said, "I'm suddenly very keen on recycling. It was one of your better ideas, Micky. I should have been more encouraging."

Much later in the day, after Max's parents had been round and taken him home, and everything had cooled down, Micky and his Dad cleared up as best they could. Micky could now see the full extent of the damage. The lawnmower and most of the tools, including many that had belonged to his Grandad, Dad's Dad, were ruined or gone completely.

Dad had built the shed himself. It had taken weeks and Micky could remember how proud he'd been when it was finished. They had eaten their tea in it that first night, in celebration. Now only the far wall was undamaged.

The whole garden was a sad mess of mud and ashes.

"Looks like something from the trenches," Dad muttered.

They were still out there when Micky just had to ask, "Why aren't you angry?"

"Wait till tomorrow. When I've calmed down I'll be really angry."

"But why aren't you angry now?"

His Dad stopped poking around under the charred remains of the workbench and came out to where Micky stood in the middle of the lawn.

He crouched down and rested his hand on Micky's shoulder. "When I got back from the Garden Centre," he said, "I saw the smoke rising from the back garden. I ran through the house, calling for you, but you weren't there. From the house it looked like the whole shed was alight. I thought you must have been inside it. When I got out into the garden you didn't answer my calls. And then I found this."

22

He stood up and took from his pocket a small, singed piece of the sleeve of Micky's sweatshirt.

"I thought this was all that was left of you."

They both stared at the piece of cloth and Micky shuddered.

"So, when Max called out and I knew that you were safe, well. . . ." He didn't finish his sentence, but Micky understood.

Neither of them spoke for a while. Then Micky said, "I'll help you build a new one."

"You're not kidding."

Micky looked again at the ruins. "We could make it bigger this time," he said. He walked forwards. By the look on his face you could tell that a Shed Project was rapidly taking shape. "Bigger. And with rooms. . . . One room for you and. . . ."

"Micky."

"Yes, Dad?"

"Don't push your luck, son."

Sammy

The Penfolds were used to Sammy disappearing. It usually happened when you'd just had words with him. Meg, who was ten, would be trying to watch a programme and Sammy, who was four, wanted to sing his latest song.

"Sammy, I'm trying to watch this. Go away."

And he would.

Or Evelyn, who was seventeen, was trying to study and Sammy was pestering her to read him a story.

"For goodness sake, Sammy. How many times do I have to say it? I'm not going to read anything to you just now. Leave me alone."

And he would.

Or Mum would come in when he had scattered the entire contents of his toy box over the living room floor.

"Sammy, you can't possibly need all your toys out at once. Tidy them up."

And Sammy would. But although he wasn't crying (he very rarely cried) you could tell from the way his mouth had gone down at the corners that as far as he was concerned he did need all his toys out at once and that as soon as he had finished tidying up he was going to disappear.

At times like this you just had to let him go. If you went after him he would shout and scream. If you tried to grab hold of him, he would struggle and kick and escape again as soon as he could.

If you left him, he'd come back again after a while. He didn't go far – his bedroom, the garden, the cupboard under the stairs, behind the settee. He'd come back in a while. Ten minutes at the most.

It was a Thursday evening in October. Mrs Penfold had come home from work to find the sink blocked.

She had cleared everything from the cupboard under the sink, so that now all the kitchen work surfaces were cluttered. The next thing was to try and undo the plastic rings that held the U-bend, she had already placed a bucket beneath this. The block would be in the U-bend. It would be a horrible mess of food scraps and her face was already screwed up against the smell that she knew would hit her as soon as it came free.

But she couldn't shift either of the rings. She sat back on the floor, sighing with annoyance.

"Evelyn! Evelyn!" she shouted. There was no reply. "Evelyn!"
"What?"

"Can you come down here a minute?" Mrs Penfold sat gazing into the cupboard until, at last, Evelyn came down.

"What?"

"Can you try and shift that?"

"Mum, I'm working."

"You've got the whole evening to work."

"I've got loads to do. It's an important assignment, it's worth a lot of points."

"What about me? How many points am I worth? Come on, have a go, it won't take a moment."

Now it was Evelyn who was sighing. She got down on her hands and knees. But she couldn't move the rings either.

"Why don't you call a plumber?" Evelyn suggested.

"Do you know how much they charge? No, what we need are some of those gripper things. Mr Tomlin's bound to have some. I'll pop round the corner and ask him. She glanced at her watch. "Keep an eye on the kids," she said, "I'll go now. We must get this fixed tonight."

"O.K." said Evelyn, already heading back up the stairs.

"The kids" included Sammy, Meg and Meg's friend Karen. Well, a sort of friend. Karen was new at Meg's school, in the same class. But Karen didn't seem like a new girl. She wasn't shy and quiet. From the first day she had been loud and bossy. It had been Karen's idea that she come round to Meg's house tonight and now Meg was wishing she'd said, "No." But it wasn't easy to say, "No," to Karen.

Meg had tried hard to suggest things they could do, games they could play. But Karen wasn't interested in any of them.

"That's boring," was all she said to each idea.

At last Meg showed Karen her penguin collection. Meg collected all sorts of penguins, she had more than thirty, from a biscuit wrapper to her favourite, which was made of cut glass. It was beautiful. If you held it to the light it was full of rainbow colours. She been collecting penguins for four years and she was proud of them. They were neatly arranged on a shelf in her bookcase.

"Why do you collect them, then?" Karen asked.

"I like penguins."

"Have you got any good videos?"

Meg was hurt. Karen hadn't even looked at them properly.

Karen was going downstairs to look for videos as Evelyn passed her going up and Mrs Penfold was pulling on her coat and opening the front door.

"Be good. Won't be long," she called. In her hurry she didn't pull the door to, but let it swing shut. The latch didn't click.

When Karen got into the living room she finally found something to amuse her. It was Sammy.

"Oh, isn't he lovely!"

Meg, who was trailing behind, stopped and smiled vaguely. She looked at her brother. It was a long time since she had thought of him in that way.

Sammy was also surprised and looked up from his truck.

"Hasn't he got big ears, though?" Karen said, and she giggled.

Meg was so relieved to find something that interested Karen that she wanted to make the most of this topic of conversation.

"He can waggle them," she said.

"Can he? Oh, go on! Waggle your ears! Go on!"

Sammy just stared at her.

"Come on, Sammy," Meg urged him, "Show Karen how

you can waggle your ears."

"Why won't he? Why won't he waggle them? Perhaps he's. . . ." here Karen became suddenly convulsed with laughter.

You can sometimes catch laughter from other people who are laughing, even if you don't know what they are laughing about. Meg caught Karen's laughter now. Both girls were soon struggling for breath. Between gasps, Karen continued. "Perhaps he's . . . . . . perhaps he's afraid . . . that if he waggles them . . . if he waggles them too much . . . he'll . . . he'll take off!"

Now they were both quite helpless. The laughter was almost silent, they were just squirming around on the settee.

Sammy stood up. His mouth had gone down at the corners, though neither of the girls noticed. He left the room.

Mrs Penfold had stopped to get fish and chips on her way back from Mr Tomlin's house.

She had tucked the warm, paper-wrapped bundles under her arm and found the key, but the door just pushed open.

"Oh," she thought to herself, "Can't have shut it properly."

She called the girls, "I can't be bothered to cook tonight. Let's eat it now while it's hot and I'll do the sink later. You lot wash your hands. Where's Sammy?" She dumped the bundles on the kitchen table and went for plates.

"Oh, he's hiding again."

Something in Meg's voice made Mum suspicious.

"What did you do?"

"Nothing. We were just having a joke."

Karen started to giggle again.

"What sort of a joke?"

Evelyn came down and into the kitchen.

"His ears!" Karen spluttered.

"What about his ears?" Mrs Penfold's voice was soft and steady but Meg knew there was danger ahead. She tried to warn Karen with a look but Karen had started to tell the rest of the story and was enjoying it, expecting Mrs Penfold and Evelyn to find it as funny as Meg had. When she finished there was silence. After a pause Mrs Penfold spoke.

"That was unkind."

There was another long pause.

"I want to go home now."

It was the quietest thing Meg had ever heard Karen say.

"Perhaps that would be best," said Mrs Penfold. "Will you walk Karen home please, Evelyn?"

No one said a word while Karen fetched her coat and Evelyn got her through the front door as quickly as possible.

Now Meg was in the kitchen, waiting for her Mum to break the silence. It wasn't until she had set the places and dished up the food that she did speak and even then she didn't look at Meg.

"How long ago was this?"

"About fifteen minutes."

"You are going to find him, young lady, say sorry and bring him for his tea."

"Yes, Mum. Sorry, Mum."

"Say sorry to *him*."

The command had released her, as if from a spell. Gladly she left the kitchen and went to look.

Meg checked Sammy's room first but he wasn't there. She went out into the garden, it was just getting dark. He wasn't in the shed, or under the fir tree. She ran back inside. He wasn't in the cupboard under the stairs. She knew he couldn't be behind the settee because the living room was where it had happened. Where else did he go? She began to call him, softly but urgently as she raced round the house. She didn't want her mother to hear the anxiety that she was beginning to feel.

She stopped. This was silly. She must slow down, look properly. Back to his bedroom. A thorough search. Under the bed. In the wardrobe. No sign.

Mum's room. No sign.

The room she and Evelyn shared. But Evelyn had been there. Check it anyway, he could have moved. Nothing.

The bathroom. But there's nowhere to hide in the bathroom. Check it anyway. No Sammy.

He definitely wasn't upstairs.

She went back downstairs. Any moment now Mum would come out of the kitchen and she still hadn't found him. She double-checked downstairs, even behind the settee. She had looked everywhere. There were no more places in the whole house that he could possibly be.

She looked through the living room window. It now seemed quite black outside, but out she went again and stood in the middle of the garden, calling him, desperately.

Like a block of ice, a terrible thought was forming inside Meg. She wanted to pretend that it wasn't there, but the thought was so big and so cold it was taking her over as she stood in the dark garden.

The thought was this. If Sammy was not in the house and he wasn't in the garden, then he must have gone out of the house, through the front door. He often tried to reach and turn the latch when Bob, the milkman, called. She had never seen him manage to open it yet, but perhaps he had grown enough now to reach it properly. And then he would go down the short front path to the gate. And then. . . .

He could be anywhere. And anyone could have found him.

"Sammy!" she wailed, "Sammy!"

Mrs Penfold came running.

"What is it? Is he hurt?"

"He's gone."

"Gone? What do you mean? He can't have gone."

"He has, he's gone. I've looked everywhere."

"Oh Meg," said Mum. "The front door. I left it open."

When Evelyn got back they all three searched the house again. Then Mrs Penfold and Evelyn went out along the street in different directions. Meg sat in the kitchen, waiting and wondering if she would ever feel normal again. When the others got back they all sat at the table, pushing away the now cold plates of fish and chips.

Mrs Penfold kept looking at her watch.

"It's my fault," Evelyn said suddenly. "You said to keep an eye on them and I didn't."

Meg said, "No, it's my fault, I. . . ."

"It doesn't matter whose fault it is," Mum interrupted fiercely but at once she reached out to her daughters. Keeping hold of their hands she said, "I'll just have to call the police."

As if those words were some sort of signal, both Meg and Evelyn began to cry at once. And joining their sobs were other sobs. They came from the cupboard under the sink.

It was hard to say which of the three outside the cupboard doors got to them first and opened them to find Sammy with his knees drawn up around the bucket beneath the U-bend. They hauled him out and he was glad enough to come. And now Mrs Penfold joined the others, with tears of relief.

"Where have you been?" she said.

Well, that was quite an easy question, even for a four-year-old. And Sammy pointed helpfully back into the cupboard as he answered, "In there."

Then they were all laughing and Sammy caught the laughter too, though he wasn't sure what he had said that was so funny.

He couldn't have put it into words but Sammy knew that sometimes it was good to be able to go away for a while. But this time it had been too long and it was even better to come back. It was better for the cupboard doors to open and to be dazzled by the kitchen light and the hugs and tears and laughter.

Not that other, hurting laughter. But this glad-to-see-you, we-were-worried-about-you-but-now-it's-all-right-again laughter.

Evelyn said, "Who wants a soggy chip?"

Fluff

He was known as Fluff. That wasn't his real name, of course. You might call your pet cat Fluff, or a cuddly toy. But it wouldn't really do for a person. Except as a nickname. And that's what it was, a nickname. He had been christened Peter Timothy Cooper. But he was known as Fluff.

It began because he was born with a little tuft of hair right in the middle of the top of his head. A little tuft of Fluff. It was a nurse who first used the name. And it stuck.

As he got older he almost forgot where it had come from. It was only a name, after all. Just like a cup is called a cup or a chair a chair. No reason, just a name. The people he'd known a long time took it for granted. Only when someone new came along would they think it was funny and ask the reason for it. That didn't happen often.

But in a way, although the original tuft had long since grown into a full head of hair, the name still suited him. It suited the kind of person he was.

If you can imagine a piece of fluff, thrown up in the air and caught by the breeze, blowing this way and that, up and down, round and round, you may get some idea of what he was like.

He never disagreed with anyone. Now, you might think that's a good thing. But it was as if he could never make up his own mind about anything. When he was talking to someone he would simply agree with whatever they said.

"What's your favourite sport, Fluff?"
"Well, I like them all. What's your favourite?"
"I like rounders best."
"Yes. I like rounders, too."

"What do you want to be when you grow up, Fluff?"
"I haven't really thought. What do you want to be?"
"I want to be a reporter."
"That sounds interesting. I think I'd like to be a reporter."

Fluff could drive his Mum to distraction.
"What do you want for your tea, Fluff?"
"I don't mind."
"Choose something."
"What is there?"
"You know what there is – what we've always got."
"Tell me anyway."
"Beefburgers, fish fingers or spaghetti."
"Um . . . what do you want?"
"I'm asking you."
"I don't mind. I like them all."
"For goodness sake, Fluff, can't you make a decision for once in your life!"
"Beefburgers then . . . or fish fingers . . . or spaghetti. I don't mind."

Although he could be infuriating, most people liked Fluff. He was certainly easy to get on with. And he never did anyone any harm.

But as he got a little older, he began to realise that he wasn't going to get through life simply by agreeing with everyone all

34

the time. For one thing, people held such different views.

Fluff was walking home from the shop with Michelle and her sister Jackie one afternoon when Michelle asked, "What's your favourite colour, Fluff?"
"Mine's blue," chimed in Jackie.
"Yes, I like blue," said Fluff.
"I like yellow best," said Michelle.
"I like yellow, too," said Fluff.
"But what's your favourite?" asked Jackie.
"They're both my favourite."
"You can't have two favourites," insisted Jackie.
"Can't you?"
Michelle persisted, "If you had to pick just one, Fluff, what would it be?"
"Well, I suppose it would be . . . a sort of . . . yellowy-blue."
"Yellowy-blue?" said both girls together.
"Yellow and blue make green," Michelle informed them knowledgeably.
"So, Fluff likes green best," concluded Jackie.
"Yes, that's right. Green's best," said Fluff, relieved that they weren't going to make him choose.

Favourite colours may not matter that much. But some things matter a lot.

The trouble began when a boy called Oliver Johnson arrived at the school. He was older than Fluff and in a different class, but Oliver noticed Fluff in the playground and soon realised that he would do pretty much anything he was told. It started in a small way.

"Fluff, can you bring your football to school tomorrow, so we can have a game?"
"Yes, Olly."
And Fluff would bring it in.

"Fluff, fetch my coat for me please."
"Yes, Olly."
And off Fluff would trot to fetch it.

"Fluff, have you got your swimming money?"

"Yes, Olly."

"Lend it to me. I'll let you have it back tomorrow."

"Yes, Olly." Fluff answered automatically. But then a troubling thought struck him. "What shall I tell my teacher

when she asks for it?"

"Just tell her you forgot," Oliver replied, shrugging his shoulders.

So he did. Fluff told her he'd forgotten his swimming money. A deliberate lie. He'd never done that before.

Oliver did pay back the money. But Fluff still felt uneasy.

Things got worse. One day Oliver took Fluff to a quiet corner of the playground and said, "I know where your teacher keeps the cooking money. It's in the third drawer down in her desk. You're going to get it for me."

Fluff didn't reply. Oliver waited. "What do you say, Fluff?" he prompted. Fluff nodded reluctantly. Oliver still wasn't satisfied. "What do you say, when someone bigger and stronger than you asks you nicely to do something?"

"Yes, Olly," Fluff mumbled.

That lunch-time Fluff crept into the classroom and stole two pounds from the cooking money.

At about this time, Fluff's Mum, his friends and his teacher all noticed the change in him. He didn't smile as much as he used to. He didn't eat as much as he used to. Instead of liking everything his Mum cooked for him, he didn't have much appetite for anything.

His Mum was getting worried. One day she sat him down and said, "Something's the matter, Fluff. Tell me what's wrong."

This time he didn't agree with her. He forced a smile and forced himself to look her in the eye as he replied, "No, there's nothing wrong, I'm fine. Really." He was getting pretty good at lying.

Fluff tried to avoid Oliver in the playground. His heart sank whenever he saw him coming towards him or heard him call his name.

"Fluff, there you are, I've been looking for you everywhere." The mock friendly voice came from behind him at the end of one lunch break when he was beginning to think that he'd escaped a whole day without being caught. There were just two minutes until the whistle. Long enough for Oliver to give Fluff his instructions.

"There's a boy in Class 3, Terry Black, do you know him?" Fluff nodded helplessly.

"He brings one pound to school every day for the tuck shop. Before he has a chance to spend it tomorrow you are going to get it."

"How?" asked Fluff wearily.

"That's your problem," replied Oliver, with that shrug of the shoulders Fluff had come to dread so much. "Just have that pound for me by lunchtime, O.K.?"

That night Fluff took himself off to bed early but hardly slept at all. Next morning, he couldn't eat his breakfast. He told his Mum he couldn't go to school, he wasn't well, he felt hot. His Mum took his temperature but it was normal. Then he said he had a tummy ache, but his Mum said that she didn't think that he was ill. She asked him again to tell her what was really the matter.

But Fluff picked up his school bag and left. His Mum

made up her mind. She would go in and speak to Mrs Marchant, the head teacher, that very day.

The vicar took assembly. He was telling them about names, how they all mean something. He knew a lot about them. He asked some of the children what their names were and wrote them up on the big flipchart, explaining where they came from and what they meant.

Then he told them about someone from the Bible, one of Jesus' friends, called Simon. Simon kept making mistakes and getting things wrong. He rushed into things without thinking. Sometimes he got too excited or too angry. He was the one who said he would never let Jesus down. But when Jesus had been arrested by the soldiers Simon was frightened and said he didn't even know him.

The vicar said that Simon was just about the last person you would ask to do a really important job, he was so unreliable. But Jesus knew he could change. He gave him the job of starting up the church. And to show how much he trusted him he also gave him a new name. Peter.

Fluff looked up. That was his name. His real name.

The vicar explained that Peter means "rock". And as he got older, Simon Peter became more and more like a rock – strong, steady, reliable.

"Is there anyone here called Peter?" the vicar asked.

Fluff shot up his hand.

"Just one," said the vicar, smiling at him. "Stand up, Peter. You have a very special name."

At break time Peter was waiting for Oliver in the playground.

"Better hurry up and find Terry," said Oliver, "he'll spend that money soon."

"It's his money. He can spend it how he likes," Peter replied steadily.

Oliver was taken aback. "I hope you're not having second thoughts, Fluff," he said, moving closer and trying to look menacing.

Peter stood his ground. "My name's Peter," he said, "and I'm not going to do it."

Oliver said nothing. He was too surprised.

"You've got to," he said at last, but it sounded feeble and he knew it.

"I won't. It's wrong." Peter was feeling stronger and stronger.

"You've got to," repeated Oliver, then he smiled. "If you don't I'll tell them about all the things you *have* done."

"No need," said Peter, beginning to walk away. "I'm going to tell Mrs Marchant myself."

"No, wait! You can't!" Suddenly Oliver was pleading with him. "They'll tell your parents." He tried to catch Fluff by the arm, but Peter shook him off.

"You'll be expelled!" Oliver called after him.

But nothing would change Peter's mind now. He walked right up to the teacher on duty and asked if he could go in to see Mrs Marchant. It was a very important matter. Something about his tone and manner convinced the teacher that she should let him go and on he walked, slowly and steadily, while Oliver looked on from a distance, his face white with terror.

The secretary said that Mrs Marchant was busy seeing someone that break time, but then she seemed to think twice, picked up the phone and buzzed through to the head's office.

She told Mrs Marchant that Peter Cooper would like to see her. When she put the phone down she said that he was to go straight in.

When he got inside, Mrs Marchant was at her desk and his Mum was sitting in a chair. He didn't even wonder what she was doing there, he just went straight towards her, arms out, and burst into tears.

It took a while for the whole business to be untangled. The grown-ups were not nearly as cross with Peter as he had

expected them to be – about the stealing and the lies. They did say that he should have told them sooner, but they weren't angry with him.

Later, Peter's Mum told him that on the morning when the trouble first came to light, she had been so furious with Oliver that she'd wanted to go onto the playground right there and then and give him what for. But now that it was over, she felt more sorry for him than anything else. At the end of term Oliver would be moving on to secondary school. She hoped that the fresh start would do him good.

The name Fluff lingered on for a while, but when people called him by his old nickname he would gently correct them: "I used to be called Fluff. But my real name is Peter."

Snow

It was the very worst time to travel on the motorway and we knew it, but had no choice. Dad couldn't leave work till five-thirty and Mum's plane from America was due in at twenty to seven. It was tipping down with rain and there was so much traffic that all three lanes were choc-a-bloc, the cars going along side by side, nose to tail.

Well, most were going along nose to tail. But my Dad's got this thing about keeping a good distance between us and the car in front. He likes to leave a lot of room. He gets really annoyed when other drivers move into the space from either side, or if the driver behind beeps him. When that happens (and it does quite often) he'll start going on about braking distances, and how a driver should always take into account the road conditions. He starts talking like the Highway Code. He goes on at us as if it's our fault.

I say "us", but it was just me on this occasion. It had been just me for some time. Mum had been away for sixteen weeks. One hundred and fifteen days to be precise. The longest we have ever been apart.

At first all the traffic was moving along at a fair speed, but when the signs said eighteen miles to go we were slowing

down. Then we came to a complete halt, crawled along for a bit and stopped again. Now the wipers sounded noisy and the rain thundered on the roof. Even though we weren't moving the wipers couldn't keep the windscreen clear.

As I watched the huge drops land I let my eyes lose focus. The screen became a blur of red and white circles from the car lights. I closed my eyes and tried to see ahead, to what it would be like in an hour or so, seeing Mum coming through customs, seeing her smile, hearing her voice.

"It's turning to sleet," Dad announced.

I opened my eyes. The drops had small, solid flecks in them. On impact with the windscreen the grains of ice exploded from the centre and began to snake their way downwards, only to be suddenly swept away by the wipers. As the minutes passed the drops were less and less of water.

"It's snow now," I said eventually.

"Don't get too excited," Dad replied, "It won't settle. Not after all that rain."

I knew he was right, but couldn't help hoping all the same. We hadn't had snow for ages. It must have been three years since the last decent fall, enough for snowballs and snowmen.

I knew snow didn't settle in these wet conditions. But then again, I'd never seen it snow like this before. It was pouring with snow. You never say that, do you? But it's the only way to describe it. Pouring with snow. When you looked at the street lights you could see it best. Huge flakes. And so many of them. More flakes than gaps in between.

And soon we saw that they *were* settling. Amazingly. They just couldn't melt quickly enough. And once they gained a foothold suddenly everything around us was bright, all the lights reflecting off the snow. So much light and the snowflakes streaming down. It was like Carnival. I started to sing to myself, quietly.

"That's all we need," sighed Dad. "Let's hope they don't divert the plane."

"Divert the plane?" The song died inside me.

"Sometimes if they can't land them safely they send the planes somewhere else, Manchester or somewhere."

"Manchester?"

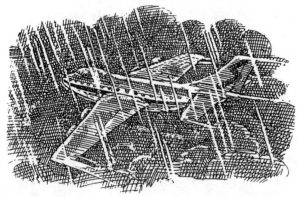

"Or somewhere."

"But what if it's snowing in Manchester?" I asked.

"Well, they'll go somewhere else."

"What if it's snowing everywhere?"

"It won't be bad everywhere."

"But what if it is? It might be. They might not be able to land at all. Not in Britain. They'll have to go back to America. Will they have enough petrol?"

"Whoa! Hold on there. Don't get yourself all worked up. Of course there'll be somewhere to land. They might not have to divert at all. Sometimes they just fly round in spirals until they've cleared the snow. They have these huge great snow ploughs, it doesn't take long. I wish I'd never mentioned it. And they don't run on petrol."

I know planes don't run on petrol. And Dad knows I know. He only said it to get me started on a different subject. But I wasn't falling for that one.

The picture of Mum was gone. All I could see now when I closed my eyes was a tiny plane, high up, going round and round above the snow clouds, with nowhere to land.

We started to move forward again. The cars were leaving dark tracks in the thin white carpet that now covered even the carriageways. "There goes another one," Dad said as a small blue car shot into the gap in front.

But up ahead, the red brake lights of the big four-by-four we had been following came on and it stopped sharply. The small blue car also tried to stop, but had no grip. It just went on and on sliding, the back of the car swinging slightly to the right as it went. It must have lasted only a moment but it felt like forever. It happened in slow motion and looked like a graceful dance. I watched open-mouthed. Then it hit, almost side on. There was a horrible dull thud followed by the sound of breaking glass.

The four-by-four pulled onto the hard-shoulder and the blue car limped after, Dad followed too. He said we'd better stop and see if we could help, they might need us as witnesses. He switched off the engine, turned up the collar of his jacket and got out.

A few minutes later he came back. He started the car and we waited a while until someone let us pull out again into the traffic.

I looked at the two parked cars as we went by. The bonnet of the blue car was all buckled up on this side. The driver was sitting in the passenger seat of the four-by-four, his head down. I couldn't see his face.

"He's only a boy," Dad said, shaking his head slowly. "He's seventeen, passed his test three weeks ago. Never driven in snow before. He's in a real state, says his Dad'll go berserk. Smashed the whole of the right wing, won't even be able to drive it home. The Jeep's hardly marked."

We were crawling along again. Dad looked at his watch and drummed his fingers on the steering wheel. Neither of us spoke for a few minutes.

I had been so looking forward to this night, I had been ticking off the days on the kitchen calendar and at last we had arrived at the date I had marked weeks ago with multi-coloured felt-tip stars. The snow had seemed to be the icing on the cake, but now it was going to ruin everything.

"Snow's a bad thing, then," I said.

Dad shot a quick glance at me. "No," he said. "Snow's not a bad thing." But he didn't sound very convincing and I needed to be convinced.

"It's bad for that man who crashed the car," I said.

No reply, even though I gave him plenty of time for one. A minute later I tried again.

"And it's bad for Mum, going round and round in the clouds."

Still no reply, but Dad shifted in his seat and fiddled with the heating controls.

"And it's bad for us, too, if we have to drive all night to get to Manchester or. . . ."

"Just hold your horses," interrupted Dad, his voice louder than it needed to be. Then more quietly, "You're doing it again. Getting yourself all worked up. Just hold your horses and let me think for a bit."

So I was quiet, looking out at the snow, now falling faster than ever. Despite everything, I wanted to be out there, scooping it up into snowballs, catching the flakes in my mouth.

After a while Dad spoke. "Snow is not a bad thing," this was better, now he sounded like he meant it. He spoke slowly and carefully, like a lawyer in court, defending his client. "Snow is wonderful. It's beautiful. It's just that sometimes it can be, well, inconvenient, even dangerous. But that doesn't make it bad. It's not snow's fault that people go rushing about in cars or want to land in aeroplanes."

"Why is it," I said, trying to be as calm and reasonable as Dad, "that most children like snow and most adults don't?"

"I don't think it's to do with *liking*," Dad replied. "It's just that most children don't have to worry about the difficulties and dangers of snow, while adults often do."

I didn't answer straight away. Usually I enjoyed our discussions. When Dad talked to me like this, it made me feel grown-up. But from what he was saying I wasn't so sure that I wanted to be grown-up. Perhaps it wasn't just snow. Perhaps this was what being an adult was all about; losing the fun of things and having instead only worries and problems.

"But Dad," I insisted, "it *is* to do with liking. You say snow is wonderful and beautiful, but do you *like* it?"

"Yes."

"Really?"

"Look, when we get back tonight," he said, "however late, if the snow lasts, you and I are going to make a snowman. All right?"

"*However* late?"

"However late."

It took us another hour to get to the airport. By then the snow had almost stopped. It turned out that Mum's flight had been late taking off and was two hours behind schedule anyway. It was now due to arrive at nine o'clock. For a short time some flights *had* been diverted elsewhere but the runways were soon cleared, just as Dad had said, and they didn't expect any more delays that night.

Dad and I had a burger and a drink at one of the airport cafés, wandered round the shops and bought a tee-shirt for Mum. It was bright red and in yellow letters it said, "WELCOME TO SUNNY ENGLAND." Then we had another drink.

At last the monitor we were watching said that the flight had landed and we went and stood near to where Mum would be appearing. I was excited and nervous, I think Dad was,

too. He kept laughing and joking about nothing in particular.

As we were standing there I had a terrible thought, that I might not recognise her. It had been such a long time that I thought I might be peering at all these faces in the crowd, not seeing her and she would walk right up to me and say, "Well, aren't you going to say, 'Hello'?" And I would look at her and she would be like a stranger to me.

But I needn't have worried. I saw her right at the other end of the hall. Both Dad and I started waving and calling.

It was wonderful to be wrapped up in the warmth of her hug. She was wearing a thick new coat. "You see," she laughed, "I came prepared." Then we gave her the tee-shirt and she laughed even more.

We didn't get home till gone eleven, but Dad kept his promise. All three of us went out onto the grass in front of our house, Mum was wearing the tee-shirt over the top of her coat. Dad kept telling us to be quiet, or we'd disturb the neighbours. We tried, but it was hard. We couldn't stop laughing.

Next morning I was up early and ran to the window. There was our snowman. Now *he* was wearing the tee-shirt and it had white shoulder-pads. So, it had snowed again during the night.

While we ate breakfast and Mum fussed over us in the kitchen, the radio was on. After the local news they read out a list of all the schools in the area that were closed. They were given in alphabetical order. My school, Westbrook, was last in the list.

"You were right, Dad," I said. "Snow is a wonderful and beautiful thing."

Lights

The letter from the Electricity Board arrived on a Thursday morning, addressed to Dad.

"Why do all the bills have my name on?" he complained as he opened the envelope. But it wasn't a bill.

"They're going to be working on the mains supply for our area, next week," Dad reported, "And on the 17th they'll have to switch the power off from 5pm for at least four hours."

"The 17th?" Mum put down the paper. "What day's that?"

"Next Tuesday."

Mum tutted. " 'The Grey Dove' is on Tuesday evenings, *and* it'll be the last episode. What time did you say?"

"Starting at five for at least four hours."

"Nine o'clock, then. My programme's at eight. I'll have to ask Helen at work to tape it for me." Mum picked up the paper again, but not for long. "And what'll we have to eat that night?"

"We could get a takeaway from the Bengal Tiger," suggested Dad hopefully.

"We're cutting down on takeaways, remember? They're too expensive."

"But this is a special occasion," said Dad.

"No. I'll do some soup on the picnic gas ring, and we can have some cheese rolls or something."

"Let's have a picnic!" chimed in Lucy. She's my sister and she's five.

"Don't be daft, it'll be dark," I said.

"So?" she replied indignantly. "You can have a picnic in the dark. You don't need lights to have a picnic. Watch!"

And to demonstrate she screwed her eyes up tight and successfully lifted the last spoonful of cornflakes from her bowl and put it in her mouth. "There!" she said triumphantly.

"But you go for a picnic on warm summer days when it's nice to be outdoors. It'll be night-time. It'll be cold," I said.

"We can all put jumpers and scarves and coats and hats on then," persisted Lucy.

Lucy seemed to have missed the whole point about picnics but I didn't know how to explain it any better.

"We can have a sort of indoor picnic," suggested Mum as a compromise.

"We must check the gas container isn't going to run out on us," said Dad. "Do you remember that time in Wales when we sat shivering in the sand dunes while it took half an hour to boil the kettle?"

"And I'll make sure we've got some candles," said Mum. "What a nuisance," she continued, "Why can't they do these things during the day? They seem to pick the most inconvenient times."

So next Tuesday, Mum, Lucy and I were all sitting round the kitchen table at five o'clock. Being winter it was already dark outside. Mum had made the rolls and the table was set but we were waiting for Dad and for the lights to go out. We had switched off all the lights in the house except in the sitting room and kitchen. When the power was cut we would leave the switches alone so that we'd know when it came back on.

Also on the table was a candle and a box of matches. Lucy was really excited. And so was I. It's hard to say why, exactly, but a power cut is something a bit different, out of the ordinary. We live down a long lane, a few minutes from the edge of town. Everything in our house works on electricity.

To lose that power is a bit like going back in time.

At about ten past five the lights went out. Lucy and I cheered.

"Light the candles!" Lucy said. "Can I start the indoor picnic?"

"Just hang on a minute." Mum felt round the table for the box of matches, which she found only after putting her hand in the pickle.

The match flared into life, with that lovely little sizzling roar. The first time the wick of the candle wouldn't light. It took a second match. The candle flame was tiny at first and looked like it might go out at any moment. But gradually, like a bud, it seemed to grow and blossom and the light it gave steadily increased.

We didn't do anything till Dad got in. We just sat there watching the flame.

"It's turned to water," said Lucy.

"Not water," I replied. "That's what happens to the wax when it gets hot, it goes clear and runny. Can you see the blue at the bottom of the flame?" I asked.

"Oh, yes," she laughed, delighted. "Blue fire!"

Sometimes the flame would grow really tall, it would start to dance and go a deep yellow, then black smoke would pour from the top. Then if you blew at it gently it would topple over, collapse and go back to normal for a while.

We knew Dad was home when the beam from the car headlights swung across the kitchen wall.

"This is cosy," he said when he came in.

Mum lit the gas ring and put the soup on.

"The picnic fire is *very* blue," observed Lucy.

"It's a beautiful night out there," Dad said. "It's really

clear. There's a bit of a moon. Going to be a frost I should think."

"I've moved the electric fire and put some kindling in the grate," said Mum. "We can have a proper fire later."

We ate our meal in silence, smiling at each other across the top of the flickering candle.

Through the window we could see stars glittering where there's normally just the pale orange glow from the town lights. The stars looked friendly and inviting, as if they wanted us to go out and play.

When we'd finished eating Dad suggested a walk down the lane. We were all keen on the idea. Mum made us wrap up well and out we went. We took a couple of torches with us. They gave an unreliable light, coming and going. We had to keep shaking them to bring the light back strongly. But even working full power they weren't much use. If they shone in your eyes it was dazzling bright, so you couldn't see anything afterwards. But if you shone them on the ground ahead or into the hedges, the thin beam just seemed to get soaked up by the darkness of the lane.

"Might as well switch them off," said Dad, "And let your eyes get accustomed to the night."

So we did. It worked. After a while the darkness began to separate into shapes and the stars in the sky were multiplying. The Milky Way was like wisps of smoke.

Ahead of us, low down, was the crescent moon. The sky around it wasn't black yet but a deep, deep blue, the last light of day. That colour seemed to bring out the beauty of the moon and the stars there. They shone and glittered like jewels on velvet.

"A bit of moon," said Lucy, echoing Dad's words from earlier. "It's a bit of fingernail."

"Oh, Lucy, it's *not* a bit of fingernail," said Mum. "It's lovely."

"Oh yes, it *is* lovely," agreed Lucy, in the voice she uses when she's explaining something that she thinks is perfectly obvious. "It's a lovely fingernail because it's God's fingernail."

"Where's the rest of Him, then?" asked Dad.

"John, don't tease her," said Mum.

"I'm not teasing. It's a serious question."

"All of Him would be too bright. A bit of fingernail's enough," was Lucy's answer.

"That's one for the book," I said.

Mum and Dad keep a book where they write down some of Lucy's sayings. Mum thinks she might be a poet when she grows up. Dad says she already is.

It used to bother me that they kept this book. They never kept one for me. I decided to ask Mum about it one day. She didn't beat about the bush. "Well," she explained, "you never really said anything very interesting. You usually spoke only when you wanted something. 'I'm hungry' or 'I need a wee.' If you did make comments about the world around you they were pretty straightforward, things like, 'Look, there's a dog.' So we never thought about making a book."

She did go on to say that I was much better at numbers than Lucy. I was always counting things.

If I could choose I think I'd rather be the one who speaks wise words, but it doesn't worry me any more. In fact I enjoy prompting Lucy with questions, waiting to see what she'll come out with. Dad's the best at asking questions. Some of the things she says really make you think. And she's only five.

"Ooh, a shooting star!" called Mum.

"Where?" demanded Lucy and I together.

"Almost right above us."

"What's a shooting star?" asked Lucy.

"It's not really a star at all," explained Mum. "It's a piece of rock from space that comes into the air around the earth and burns up."

"I thought it was cold up there," I said.

"It is," continued Mum, "But because the air is thick, compared with space, it sort of rubs against the rock and heats it up."

"Will there be another one?" Lucy asked.

"Perhaps. But you'll have to be patient."

We all stood still in the lane, heads craned back until they ached. Lucy thought she saw one, but it was a plane; a little cluster of different coloured lights, some flashing, a tiny constellation that moved slowly across the sky, blotting out stars as it went. Not until it was well across the sky did we hear the low rumble of it.

After a couple of minutes Dad said, "Come on you lot, I'm cold. Let's get that fire started." And he and Mum began to walk slowly back along the lane. But Lucy and I were determined and at last we were rewarded. Just a small shooting star, and lower down in the sky, but we both called out together so we knew we hadn't imagined it. Then we ran along the lane to find Mum and Dad. Our eyes were so used to the dark now that we could see well enough to run.

Back at home Dad lit the gas ring again and put the kettle on for a cup of tea. Mum lit the fire. Once that got going it made the sitting room quite bright, we didn't need candles as well. We hardly ever have a real fire, but whenever we do Mum always says that we ought to make the effort more often.

54

Just as we had sat around the candle earlier now we sat beside the fire. A fire has most of the good points of a candle – the shifting, flickering light, the blue flames, but also some extra features of its own – a wider range of colours, sound effects, a lovely smell of woodsmoke and the heat.

Of course – heat. That's the whole point isn't it? We stretched out our hands towards it.

"It's time for bed, Lucy," said Mum. But we all knew she was just saying it out of habit. No one moved.

And then the main light came on above us. Hard, dazzling light that hurt our eyes.

"Oh, someone, switch it off," said Dad, his hands covering his face.

I got up and turned both the sitting room and kitchen lights off and came back to the fire.

"What time is it?" asked Mum.

Dad peered at his watch in the firelight. "Quarter to eight. They're early. You'll be able to watch your programme, after all."

But Mum, who was sitting on the rug, just rested her head back, eyes closed, against Dad's chair and said, "Let's just stay like this. I can watch it any time now Helen's recording it."

And so we did.

"Guess how many different lights we've seen tonight, while the power's been off," I said.

The others went through them, calling them out. It took them ages to get all twelve, even with the three of them working together.

Special Things

All term the children had been bringing things into class. Special Things. Not valuable, necessarily, except to their owners. On Tuesday mornings, when the register had been taken, the whole class squeezed into the book corner, where they sat on the cushions while two or three of the children would show the others what they'd brought in and say why it was special to them.

Now it was nearly the end of term and everyone had brought in something. Everyone except Morna. Miss Peters had reminded Morna several times. It didn't have to be anything much. What about a cuddly toy or a favourite book?

But Morna would just shake her head and look sad. Morna always looked sad. She had been at the school for two years now but had never really settled. She didn't say much and when she did she spoke with a different accent, which, if anything, had become stronger and more difficult to understand since she had arrived. At first some of the other children had tried to be friendly, but Morna did little to encourage them.

When they asked her to join in a playground game she would say no, she might scuff her shoes and get into trouble.

When they asked her if she would like to join one of the school Clubs she would say no, she couldn't read music, was too short for netball and useless at making things.

Some of the children in her class had invited her to their parties, but she hadn't turned up.

She expected the worst. And the worst seemed often to happen. She expected to do badly at everything. She expected her stories to be dull and usually they were. She expected to get her sums wrong and mostly she did. She expected to come last in running races, so she would stop trying half way through – and come last.

And even on the brightest of summer days she always wore a coat to school.

One break time, in the playground, someone said, "Not Morna, more like Moaner." The others laughed and Morna had acquired a nickname. After a while the teachers got to hear about it and said that the name-calling must stop. It did, but Morna went on being different, an outsider.

Which is why Miss Peters particularly wanted Morna to bring in something to share with the class. But it was getting near to the end of term and still she hadn't.

There were just two Tuesdays left when one of the children

58

suggested that Miss Peters herself should bring in a Special Thing. Everyone said, "Yes, Miss, you too. You bring something."

Miss Peters smiled and said that she would.

The following Tuesday morning Surinder was reading a new book. Her brother had bought it for her. It was called "How To Be A Detective". It was all about breaking codes, identifying fingerprints and searching for vital clues. Surinder was enthralled. She had already decided to award the book the maximum ten out of ten when she came to do her review.

Surinder's interest in detection had begun a few months before, with a documentary she had watched on T.V. about a real life private eye. And now she watched as many programmes and read as many books on the subject as she could, both fact and fiction. Her greatest hero was Sherlock Holmes. She wanted to be a detective herself when she was older.

So Surinder was disappointed when Miss Peters told them all to stop reading, it felt as if they hadn't had nearly as long as usual. But then she remembered that Miss Peters was going to show them what she'd brought in, so she quickly got ready. She could read some more during the dinner break.

When they were all settled in the book corner, Miss Peters opened her bag and produced a small black box, made of some kind of metal. It was plain except for the hinged lid.

The lid was decorated with small pieces of mother-of-pearl. The fragments glittered pink and green as the children passed it round. The way the colours shifted in those little pieces of shell, it was as though you were looking right down into them, as if they went deep into the box. No one wanted to let it go, but impatient hands were always reaching for it.

"It's a snuffbox," explained Miss Peters. "Snuff is a powder made from tobacco. Snuff-taking is uncommon these days but in the past people used to take snuff. It was a fashionable habit for gentlemen."

"Whose was it?"

"Is it old?"

"It belonged to my Grandad. The box is empty but it still smells of snuff."

"Can I open it, Miss?" asked Nimal who was holding it at that moment.

Miss Peters nodded.

From then on everyone who took the box, looked at the mother-of-pearl on the lid and then opened the lid. It smelt musty and sort of warm, like old clothes.

"When did he give it to you?" Surinder asked.

"Well, he didn't, exactly. When he died and we were clearing out his things, I found it. My mother knew that I was fond of it and said that I should be the one to keep it."

The box continued on its journey. Everyone held it carefully, as if it were very fragile. At last it got back to Miss Peters. She, too, looked at the lid then lifted the box to her face and closed her eyes.

"Smell is a very powerful thing," she said, her eyes still closed. "It is the first sense to develop. A smell can trigger off strong memories, it can take you right back to something that has happened in the past. When I smell this box, it takes me back to when Grandad was alive and I was little. I see him in his thick grey suit. He used to wear his suit even when we went to the seaside."

She was speaking as if she were a long way away. It was quiet. Nobody moved. Nobody spoiled the quietness. Some of the children had also closed their eyes as if they were sharing the picture of Miss Peters' Grandad in their

minds, seeing him on the beach in his thick grey suit.

Then she closed the box with a small snap and the spell was broken.

"Morna's crying, Miss," said Surinder.

"Again," someone murmured.

Miss Peters silenced them and went over to talk to Morna as the others got up and went back to their places.

"But we haven't smelt the box yet," complained one of the first children to have seen it, before Nimal opened the lid.

"I'll leave it on my desk for the rest of the day and if you all promise to be very careful you can have a look – and a smell – when you get a spare moment."

So that's what happened. Miss Peters took a piece of shiny blue cloth from the material tray, draped it over a small pile of books for a plinth and made a label about snuff.

After dinner, Surinder got chatting to some of her friends and didn't remember her book until half way through the break. Then she asked a dinner lady if she could go back indoors to fetch it. When she got to the cloakroom, Morna was sitting on the bench among the coats. When Morna saw Surinder approaching she hurriedly stuffed something into her pocket.

"What are you doing?" asked Surinder.

"Nothing." Morna stood up and walked off. Surinder

caught a glimpse of shiny blue material sticking out from her pocket.

Surinder walked along the empty corridor and opened the classroom door. The pile of books was still there on Miss Peters' desk, but the box and the cloth were gone.

Surinder's first impulse was to go and tell Miss Peters at once. But then she decided to think her discoveries through for herself. There were a few minutes before the end of play. She wouldn't need her book to occupy her now, she had her own case to solve. She went back outside. She just had to piece together all the clues.

Who was the only person who hadn't brought a Special Thing to school? Morna.

Perhaps Morna hadn't got anything Special of her own.

Suddenly Surinder remembered that Morna had cried this morning. She must have been crying because she was the only person in the class not to have a Special Thing.

Morna was jealous. Jealousy was the motive for the crime. And when Miss Peters left the box on her desk she had the perfect opportunity.

Morna had the motive and the opportunity. The vital clue

was that Surinder had seen her acting suspiciously in the cloakroom with the piece of blue material.

That wasn't just evidence, it was proof. Morna was guilty.

Surinder was sure that a quick search of Morna's coat pocket later on would reveal the box wrapped up in the blue material. For the time being, though, she would tell no one.

She felt a deep sense of satisfaction in having solved so quickly her first case – The Case of the Missing Snuffbox – and was glad when the whistle went for the end of play.

When the children came back indoors, word spread rapidly that the box had been taken. Miss Peters followed the class in and stood by the blackboard.

"After lunch someone came to find me and tell me that the snuffbox had gone." She was very calm and didn't sound angry, but a bit sad. "I think there must be someone in our class who knows what has happened. Perhaps someone has borrowed it to have a look and not put it back yet," she said. "Perhaps someone has accidentally damaged it and is worried that they will get into trouble. Well, I won't be cross, so long as you come and tell me. You can talk to me after school. Now we'll get on with our work."

Surinder put her hand up,

"What is it, Surinder?"

"It's about the box, Miss."

"If you know anything, come and talk to me privately later on."

But Surinder couldn't wait. This would be her moment of triumph, like the end of a whodunnit. This was the proper time and place for a detective to reveal the truth, with all the possible culprits sitting round in a room together. In this case, however, there was no need to discuss any other suspect, she just came right out with her verdict.

"It was Morna," she announced and pointed her finger dramatically.

But far from being pleased with this deduction, now Miss

Peters really was angry. "How dare you accuse someone like that. Come outside, I want to talk to you, young lady. And Morna, dear, you'd better come, too. The rest of you read your books and I don't want to hear a sound."

Miss Peters led the two girls, Morna crying, out into the corridor. At that moment, Mr Marsh, the deputy, came up. "Spot of bother?" he asked cheerfully, but was in too much of a rush to wait for the reply. "Here's your snuffbox, Miss Peters. Popped in to your room earlier for some dictionaries, saw it on your desk. Borrowed it to show my class. We're doing Walter Raleigh, tobacco and all that, hope you don't mind. Must dash, choir practice in the hall. Thanks." And off he went.

The three of them stood for a moment looking at the box in Miss Peters' hand. At last she spoke to Surinder, "It looks as though we've both been a bit hasty. Wait there," she said and walked off down the corridor. While they waited Surinder couldn't bring herself even to look at Morna.

Miss Peters returned with Mrs Hodge, the head teacher. For one terrible moment, Surinder thought that Miss Peters was going to tell Mrs Hodge that she had accused Morna of stealing, but actually Miss Peters had asked her to mind the class for a few minutes. She wanted to take the two girls to the staffroom, for a little chat, to try to sort things out.

Sitting in one of the big armchairs, Surinder heard how, after lunch, Morna had gone into the classroom to fetch her scarf and discovered that the snuffbox had disappeared. Then Morna had come straight here, to the staffroom, to tell Miss Peters. They both returned to the classroom to search. Morna had been very upset.

While they were searching, Morna told Miss Peters how much she wished she had a Special Thing to bring in. She had had several ideas. On one Tuesday she had even brought something to school – a tartan Biro with "I love Edinburgh" inscribed in gold letters, a holiday souvenir. But in the end she hadn't dared to show them. It was, after all, she said, such an ordinary Thing. She was sure all the other children would laugh. She knew none of them liked her.

Surinder felt ashamed when she heard that.

That morning, when Miss Peters had been telling the class about her Grandad, Morna had begun to think about her own Grandad. She hadn't seen him for ages. Not since her Mum had brought her to live here, a long way from home. She still didn't really understand why they'd had to leave so suddenly and why they hadn't been able to go back and visit the people she used to know, the friends and relatives. As the snuffbox was being passed round Morna remembered that her Grandad had given her an old penny. It was thinking about him that had made her cry.

As they searched the classroom, Miss Peters asked if Morna still had the penny. Yes, it was in her money box. Miss Peters said that it would be the perfect thing to bring in.

"But it's just an old penny. It isn't even shiny and it's worn almost smooth," Morna had told her.

Miss Peters had picked up the piece of blue material and given it to Morna. "Now," she said, "get a small box, scrumple up this material, and put it inside with the penny on top. You'll be amazed what a difference a bit of presentation can make."

So, Miss Peters had given that piece of cloth to Morna.

Surinder felt even more ashamed when she heard this. "I am sorry Morna," was all she could say. She was beginning to see why Morna always felt sad and lonely. She also knew that she was partly to blame.

"You will bring your penny in, won't you?" she urged.

"But what if I can't find a box?"

"Oh, Morna, dear, do try to look on the bright side for once." Even kind Miss Peters couldn't keep all the impatience out of her voice.

"But don't you remember *my* Special Thing?" Surinder asked excitedly. It had been right at the beginning of term. She had been one of the first in the class to bring something to school. It was a gift her cousin had sent her from India. Both Miss Peters and Morna tried to think back. At last

Morna's face brightened. In fact she smiled. "It was a little wooden box," she said.

Long Division

Max was worried. Today was a big day for him. In the evening his favourite football team would be playing one of the best clubs in the whole of Europe. Much as he admired and believed in his team, he knew that it was going to be a tough match.

Yes, Max was very worried. And there was no one with whom he could share his worry. Even Micky, his best friend, couldn't fully appreciate the situation.

"What's up with you then?" Micky asked when they had walked a hundred metres in gloomy silence on their way to school that morning.

"You wouldn't understand," sighed Max.

"Try me," replied Micky.

"O.K." Max stopped walking. "Tonight, United are playing San Batista in the second leg of the Cup Winners' Cup Quarter Finals and they need to win by a margin of at least two goals to qualify on goal difference."

"You were right," said Micky. "You're on your own for this one."

Really, how could he be expected to think about anything else? No one should have to work today. It should have been declared a National Holiday. People should be completely free to concentrate on the problems facing United and to discuss them over a leisurely milk shake down at the local burger bar.

All this thought and discussion would be bound to result in some great ideas. Somewhere in the country, someone would be nipping out of a burger bar every few minutes to the nearest phone box, to ring through their suggestion to Billy Watkins, United's manager. There would be no charge for these calls.

That's what would happen if Max had anything to do with it.

But here was Mrs Blake trying to teach them Long Division. Long Division, for goodness sake. What was the point? Didn't she know that the calculator had been invented?

Everyone in the class had been given a piece of paper to practise on. Mrs Blake had been through several examples on the board and everyone was supposed to be having a go.

When Max received his piece of paper he wrote down the title, 'Long Division Practice' and began to work furiously, but not at Long Division. A plan had come to him. It involved all eleven United players standing for the entire match on their own goal line, jumping up and down alternately so that it was simply impossible for the other team to score.

That just left the problem of United scoring two goals themselves – but one thing at a time.

He was putting the finishing touches to his TOTAL DEFENCE STRATEGY and wondering whether Billy Watkins' number would be in the phone book, when Mrs Blake said, "It's time to pack away now. I hope you've all got the idea because I'm giving you each a sheet of Long Division sums to do tonight."

"Yeah, wicked!" said Peggy Baxter next to him.

"Poor Peggy Baxter," sneered Max, "So weird. So sad." But Peggy was used to Max. She didn't even bother to reply. She was too busy clearing her desk so that her table would be first to get the question sheets.

Only then did Max look at the board and the last example that Mrs Blake had done for them.

There were numbers everywhere. Max could make out the division box, but what was this cascade of numbers below it? And what were those little multiplications doing, orbiting the main sum? Could this really be just one of them – all those numbers for one Long Division?

"Don't look so worried, Max. I can see you've done lots of practice. With those to help you, you'll remember what to do," said Mrs Blake.

Max quickly folded his piece of paper and put it in his pocket.

"And I want these sheets back first thing tomorrow," said Mrs Blake as she began to hand them round.

The first part of the evening was taken up with eating tea and trying to solve the problem of how United were going to score two goals. Inspiration was slow to arrive so Max decided instead to review the TOTAL DEFENCE STRATEGY. When he fished the piece of paper from his jacket pocket he also found the sheet of sums Mrs Blake had given them. He groaned. There were just fifteen minutes until the live broadcast of the match began on telly.

"Dad, can you help me with my maths?"

"Sorry, Max, I've got a meeting tonight, I've got to go out in a few minutes. Ask Mum."

"Mum, can you help me with my maths?"

"Sure. What are you doing?"

"Long Division."

"Ooh, right. Well, we might need the big table in the dining room. Long Division is serious stuff."

"Can't we work in here?"

"If you like. Switch the telly off, then."

"But Mum. . . ."

"What?"

"The match is on in a moment."

"But you just asked me to help you with some maths?"

"Yes, but . . . we could have the telly on too, with the sound down."

"No, Max. You know that wouldn't work. You can't concentrate on two things at once. I'll gladly help you, but the telly goes off. Why not record the match and watch it tomorrow?"

"No. No thanks. It doesn't matter."

"What do you mean, 'It doesn't matter'?"

"It doesn't matter. I'll do the sums tomorrow. There's no hurry."

Max went upstairs. Tony, his brother, was in his room, doing his homework and listening to music with his headphones on.

"Tony?"

"What?"

"I'll clean your bike."

"What?" Tony took off his headphones.

"I'll clean your bike. At the weekend."

"Why?"

"If you do some sums for me."

"Oh." Tony smiled. "Do them *with* you, you mean."

"No. Do them *for* me." Max mumbled, looking down at his slippers.

"This wouldn't be something to do with a certain football match, would it?"

Max ignored the question. He knew Tony knew the answer already. "Will you?" he asked.

"It's against the rules."

"Please, Tony. You can explain it all to me at the weekend."

"Thanks."

"I've got to watch the game. You know I have."

Max paused. Tony didn't reply. Time was running out, Max decided to press on with his instructions. "It's Long Division. If you do them on another piece of paper then I can copy them up later, but you'd better do about three wrong so that Mrs Blake isn't suspicious."

"Max, this is organised crime."

Max feared he'd pushed too hard. He said nothing but put on his most pathetic, pleading expression.

Tony sighed. "I'll tell you what. I'll do the sums, with the working out. I'll even write notes to explain what I've done. You never know, you might learn something. If you want to change the answers, that's up to you. But all this is going to cost you not one, not two but three bike cleans. And. . . ."

Max could now hear the music that signalled the start of the sports coverage and was becoming frantic with impatience.

"Thanks, Tony. Yes, anything, I'll do anything, but I really have to go now. . . ."

"Wait, just a moment," insisted Tony. "It's important we agree conditions."

"I said I'll do anything," wailed Max, and he meant it. Right then he would have agreed to a lifetime of bike cleaning.

"The first cleaning will take place this weekend and the other two at any time that I request within the next month. I'll draw it up in writing for you to sign later. Is that acceptable?"

"Yes, yes." Max had turned in the doorway now.

"And it had better gleam!" Tony called after him.

"It will, it will," Max replied as he bounded down the stairs.

The next afternoon, Mrs Blake handed back the marked sheets.

"That was excellent, Peggy. All correct. And you even made up some more of your own to do. Well done."

Max mimed being sick while Mrs Blake's back was turned, making some of the other children giggle. Mrs Blake wheeled round at once, but she looked pleased.

"And all correct from you too, Max. You see, I told you

not to worry."

"Oh no!" Max thought to himself. After the match last night his Mum had insisted that he went straight to bed. He was too depressed to care about his homework then, anyway. And this morning he had been in such a rush that he just copied the sums Tony had done straight onto the sheet. He had forgotten to make some of them wrong. He blushed and looked embarrassed, but not for the reason everyone supposed, as Mrs Blake handed him his paper and kept smiling at him for rather longer than he liked.

The day after that was Friday. Mrs Blake was taking assembly. She had got some props at the front: an easel with a piece of black paper and a box of chalks, a football and the blackboard on wheels from the Music Room.

She said she was going to need three helpers. Everyone shot their hands up in the air. But she said, "No, you can all put your hands down. I've already decided who I'm going to ask, because I know that they have some special skills. I want Fiona Clarke, John Thompson and Max Wallace."

Max scrambled to his feet and made his way to the front with the other two. Fiona was brilliant at art and John was probably the best footballer in the school. Mrs Blake had moved across to the blackboard and had begun to write. At the top of the board, leaving plenty of space underneath, she set out a sum, a long division sum. Two thousand nine hundred and fifty-five divided by sixty-eight.

Max went very pale.

"You come and stand over here, Max," said Mrs Blake, "We'll get to you in a moment." Max moved reluctantly over to the blackboard and stood looking as though he really didn't mind if Mrs Blake forgot him forever.

"Now, Fiona is very good at art," continued Mrs Blake in her cheery assembly voice. "Would you draw us a picture, Fiona? You're good at rabbits, aren't you? Will you draw us a rabbit?"

Fiona began at once.

"We'll leave Fiona with her picture and move on. John is very good at football. John can bounce the ball on his head, chest, knees and shoulders for quite a long time. Infants, move back and make a bit more space for him. There, that's it. Go on John, have a go."

John's first try wasn't too successful. But Mrs Blake was encouraging. "It's difficult in the hall, when you're used to having as much space as you want outside. Try again, John."

His second attempt was much better, he kept the ball up for ages and drew a warm round of applause from the school.

When the applause had died down (and one of the teachers had picked her way along a line of Infants to sort out some who kept clapping for too long) Mrs Blake continued, "Let's go back to Fiona and see how she's getting on. Oh, that's lovely, dear. See how she's using lots of different chalks together to get the colours she wants?"

Another ripple of applause began, but Mrs Blake raised her hand and said that they would give Fiona a clap at the end, when she had finished completely.

"Now, let's move on to Long Division." A little gasp went up from the School. They didn't know what Long Division was but it looked and sounded awful.

Max was feeling positively sick by now. Mrs Blake came and stood beside him. "In our class we've just begun to learn how to do these sums."

This was it. She was now going to tell the School that Max was good at Long Division, that he had down a whole sheet of them and made no mistakes at all. Then she would ask him to do the one on the board. And he wouldn't even be able to start. He hadn't got a clue. Not a clue.

"Here's a piece of chalk for Max." Mrs Blake pushed a long, brand new piece of chalk into Max's sweating palm and paused for a moment. Max looked up at her, waiting for the command. She met his look and winked. Did she? Or was he imagining? She winked again.

She knew! She knew he'd cheated!

For just a little longer she made him sweat, before saying, in her bright, cheery, assembly voice, "But of course, if you've only just started to learn about something it's very difficult to manage on your own. Isn't it, Max?"

He only nodded, but so fiercely everyone laughed.

"So when we're learning, it's really good to have someone to work with us. Isn't it, Max?"

"Oh yes, Mrs Blake. It is. It is!" his nods seemed to say.

"Well then, shall we ask someone up to help you? Shall we ask, let's see, shall we ask Peggy Baxter?"

"Oh yes, yes, yes! Let's ask Peggy Baxter!" he nodded.

"Come on then Peggy, come and work with Max to solve this sum."

Peggy came up and stood with Max, she whispered to him and he wrote down whatever she told him. It looked like they were working together but it was all Peggy. Max could only think about how he was never, ever going to be rude to Peggy again.

Had Mrs Blake known? Or was it just coincidence? At break time, as the class was leaving the room, Mrs Blake called Max back.

"You handed this in with your homework sheet yesterday." She held out the sheet of paper which had the title 'Long Division Practice' but which was covered with writing and diagrams for the TOTAL DEFENCE STRATEGY. He felt his face burn bright red.

"Not a bad idea," Mrs Blake went on. "Pity you didn't let Billy Watkins know, might have made all the difference. Disappointing game, wasn't it?"

"Yes," said Max.

Mrs Blake went back to her marking. But Max lingered at her desk. After a while she looked up again.

"Can I help you, Max?"

"I cheated, Mrs Blake."

"Yes, Max." She put down her pen. "I'm going to go and get my coffee. Have several sheets of rough paper and a sharp pencil ready when I get back."

"Shall I get my homework sheet, as well?"

Mrs Blake looked surprised. "Oh no, we won't need that. Long Division can wait. First, you and I must sit down and see if we can work out what went so wrong for United in the second half."

Plan 4

It was a donkey with a big, floppy hat on its head. The donkey's long ears poked through the hat. It was made of shiny pottery. Uncle Bob had brought it back from Spain. Now it was in the place where it was going to live, on the mantelpiece.

Jenny wasn't supposed to touch the things on the mantelpiece. They were all fragile things. They were mostly porcelain figures, some of them very old and so delicate they looked like they'd fall apart if you so much as breathed on them.

When Jenny first grew tall enough to reach it and see what was on it, the mantelpiece had held a strange and dangerous fascination. The fascination of a cliff edge. She felt herself powerfully drawn towards the objects there.

Sometimes she had not been able to resist reaching out her hand. But the cold, shiny surfaces might have been fire, for at the first touch she would snatch back her hand and stare, wide-eyed at the forbidden figures, wondering when she would be old enough to be trusted to hold them.

Now that she *was* older, she had rather lost interest, the figures had become familiar and taken for granted.

But last week Uncle Bob had stayed overnight on his way home from his Spanish holiday and he had brought them each back a present. Uncle Bob always had a theme for his presents. This year the theme was donkeys. For Dad there was a bar of soap in the shape of a donkey, its body round like a barrel, with no neck and stubby little legs. It was still in its polythene wrapping in the bathroom cabinet.

For Jenny, some notepaper with a different drawing of a donkey in the top lefthand corner of every sheet.

The pottery donkey was for Mum.

It wasn't so much the shiny smoothness and bright colours that attracted Jenny now, but the desire to know the answer to a simple question, a question that had been troubling her ever since Uncle Bob had produced the pottery donkey, carefully wrapped in a tee-shirt, from his travel bag. The question was: Does the donkey's hat come off?

Jenny was on her own in the sitting room, waiting for her Mum to finish her coffee in the kitchen before taking her to school. She hadn't actually planned anything but this was obviously the perfect moment. She glanced towards the door which was nearly shut and crept over to the fireplace.

There was the donkey, standing behind the shepherdesses and elegantly dressed ladies. It looked a bit odd. Rather heavy and lumpy in comparison, and with a very unrealistic grin on its face. Donkeys don't grin, do they?

Jenny wondered what her Mum really thought of it. When Uncle Bob had unwrapped it from the tee-shirt she had sounded quite delighted. But you can never tell with grownups.

She remembered the new picture at Sue and Brian's house. One time they'd all gone over there for a barbecue and Sue had just bought a picture. It hung, in pride of place, in their front room. Mum and Dad went on and on about how much they liked it. But later, as soon as they got in the car to come home, they went on and on about how awful it was.

Jenny reached forward, fingers outstretched.

"Ooh, cold," she whispered to herself, drawing back her hand at the first touch. But this time she was determined. It now seemed like the most important question in the world: Does the donkey's hat come off? She listened. The radio was still on in the kitchen, Mum wouldn't be finished for a while yet.

Her hand went out again and this time grasped the donkey round the middle and lifted it down. Her palm felt sweaty and slippery. She held it very firmly.

She knew better than to turn it upside down, she didn't want to tip the hat onto the floor. Instead she raised it up so that she could look under the brim of the hat, where it joined the donkey's head. There was a definite line that ran around the bottom of the hat. A crack. A gap.

She tried shaking the donkey gently, to see if the hat wobbled on top of its head, but it didn't. She was reluctant to take hold of the hat itself. It looked almost as flimsy as the straw it was supposed to represent. But if she were going to know the answer to her question she had no choice. Still gripping the body of the donkey tightly with her left hand she took hold of the brim of the hat between thumb and forefinger of her right and tried, very gently, to wiggle it. It seemed quite firm. She tried the opposite side. It still didn't move.

Perhaps it would only come off if you lifted evenly, all round the brim. She changed her grip, positioning her fingers around and under the brim of the hat, with the top of the hat cupped in the palm of her hand. She gave it a really good tug.

Yes! The hat did come off! Jenny gave a small, satisfied laugh. She was about to take it through to show Mum, whom she was sure would forgive her for getting it down from the mantelpiece when she saw the wonderful discovery that Jenny had made. But then she looked again.

Something was wrong.

Still poking through the yellow hat that rested in the palm of her right hand, were the two, large grey ears. And when she looked at the donkey in her left hand, she saw that the top of its head was now a jagged lump of raw, white pottery.

"Ready?" called her Mum from the hall.

Jenny jumped but held on to the two pieces. She just had time to stand the donkey on the shelf and balance the hat on top before her Mum put her head round the door to call her again.

Jenny was unusually quiet on the way to school. Mum thought she must be worrying about the tables test she was having that day.

Jenny's teacher thought she must be ill. She looked pale and couldn't concentrate. She hardly spoke to anyone all day. When the class was trying to come up with a list of jungle animals for their Tropical Island Project, with Mrs Winters standing at the board, writing them down, Jenny was staring anxiously out of the window.

"Come on, Jenny," said Mrs Winters. Jenny started guiltily at the sound of her name. "You give us an animal."

"Donkey," blurted Jenny. Everyone laughed.

What could she do? What *could* she do?

By lunch time she had so many different ideas jostling for space in her head that she couldn't think about any of them properly. After nibbling at her packed lunch, she left the hall, took her notebook from her desk and sat on a bench hidden among the coats in the cloakroom. Perhaps having things in black and white would help. She would write them down.

PLAN 1: DO NOTHING

Advantage: The donkey might not be discovered for a long time. (No one in our house is very keen on dusting).

Disadvantage: I will never know when the Terrible Day Of Discovery will arrive. How many days like this can I stand?

PLAN 2: WHEN I GET HOME TONIGHT ARRANGE THE PIECES ON THE FLOOR NEAR THE FIREPLACE AND BLAME FLUFF (THE CAT)
Advantage: The cat gets the blame.
Disadvantage 1: Will anyone believe that the cat managed to pick out the donkey from in amongst all the figures and knock it to the floor without disturbing any of the others?
Disadvantage 2: This will involve lying which will only make things worse if they don't believe the bit about the cat.

PLAN 3: REMOVE THE EVIDENCE COMPLETELY
Advantage: No broken pieces to be discovered!
Disadvantage: Mum is going to notice straight away. (This plan is no use at all, I don't even know why I bothered to write it down. Except that it puts off writing PLAN 4)

PLAN 4: I can't bear to write it down. Mum's going to be so cross when I tell her.

Well, Jenny was brave. As soon as she got home she put PLAN 4 into operation. At once a huge weight was lifted from her. All day long she had been carrying this weight around. It was made of guilt and secrecy and hiding and fear and the lies she nearly told.

The funny thing was, Mum wasn't upset about the donkey in the slightest. She gave Jenny a hug and said how pleased she was that she had told her about it. Then she went through to the other room, brought back the donkey and the hat and put them straight in the bin.

Jenny was a bit surprised. "Perhaps we could mend it with glue," she suggested, looking down at the hatless, earless donkey, still grinning up at her from among the potato peelings.

"That wouldn't work," said Mum, chopping up the potatoes.

"Why not?"

"Because we haven't got all the pieces."

"What do you mean?"

"Well, this morning I hoovered up quite a few little bits of pottery that were lying on the floor by the fire."

"You knew then," said Jenny quietly. "Just as well I didn't try to blame Fluff."

Mum smiled.

"But what shall we tell Uncle Bob? He might ask where it is next time he's here," Jenny said.

Mum thought for a moment. "We could always blame the cat."

"That would be lying," said Jenny in a voice so solemn that Mum stopped chopping the potatoes and turned round.

"You're quite right, love," she said.

It didn't take long for Jenny to reach the same conclusion as she had earlier in the day.

"It'll have to be Plan 4 again," she said, heading out of the kitchen and towards the stairs. This time, though, she was quite looking forward to it. Telling the truth to Mum had given her such a wonderful feeling of relief, and now she could enjoy the experience all over again.

"What's Plan 4?" her Mum called after her.

"I'm going to write to Uncle Bob," Jenny said, beginning to climb the stairs. "And tell him the truth."

She stopped at the top of the stairs, another idea had just occurred to her. "I'll use his donkey notepaper," she shouted down. "It'll be perfect. I'll draw a hat on one of the donkeys and with a few arrows I can show him exactly what happened."

Wildworld

"Simon is always keen to join in class discussions."

That's what his last school report had said. Simon had been pleased, it sounded like a point in his favour.

But his Dad said it just meant he talked too much, only the teacher was too polite to come right out and say it. Especially as the report went on, "though he must try harder to listen carefully to others."

Simon did do a lot of talking, he would be the first to admit that. But there were so many things in the world that needed talking about.

Simon didn't really have conversations with other people. Being with him was more like having the radio on – he talked and you listened. But, unlike a radio, which will carry on just as cheerfully in an empty room, Simon enjoyed having an audience. It was nice to have someone to nod or smile in the right places.

Anyone who turned into School Lane at the same time as Simon on a weekday morning would be treated to something like this:

"I'm getting my new trainers tonight, they're dead cool, mainly white with silver stripes, they're in the window at Dobson's, have you seen them? King Brawn on The Power Game had a pair just like them. Did you watch it? Do you think he shaves his head, or is he just bald? I'm not going to shave at all when I'm older, are you? My Dad spends hours shaving, what a waste of time. Why doesn't Tarzan ever have a beard? I mean you can't imagine him shaving every morning, can you? And where would he get the razors? Unless it's something to do with diet. Perhaps if you eat bananas all the time you lose the ability to grow a beard. I could find out, Grandad brought us this huge crate of bananas back from the market last night, the stall holder was practically giving them away, seeing as how it was last thing before the market closed. Looks like we'll be living on bananas for weeks. I'll watch Dad closely. I gave some banana to my fish, just as an experiment, to see if they liked it but I don't think they did. Do you like bananas? I mushed some up and dropped it in the tank, it stayed together as a lump and sank straight down and into the treasure chest in the pebbles at the bottom. The fish swam around the chest and had a good look but they didn't touch it. It was still there this morning. Grandad got the treasure chest from the market, too. You can get some real bargains if you know which stalls to look at. He's seen a pair of trainers just like the ones I want and he's taking me there first tonight to see if they are the same. If so they'll be much cheaper than from the shop. But you have to be careful 'cos sometimes they make them look the same but they're not really. Even the name of the make is almost the same with just one letter different or something but I'll recognise if they are or not, I've memorised them from the window of Dobson's, have you seen them? They're dead cool."

The questions were thrown in as an attempt to keep the listener interested enough to stay around, but if they were ever answered Simon didn't appear to notice.

The other children on Simon's table at school had grown

used to working with a running commentary throughout the day. On the occasions when he was away it seemed unnaturally quiet. Just lately, when they were doing the Romans, Simon had decided to learn the Roman names for as many British towns as possible. These names were so much better than their modern equivalents. Take LONDINIUM, for example. How much grander and more like a capital city it sounded than London.

Or ISCA DUMNONIORUM. That was Exeter.

Or VENTA BELGARUM, which was Winchester.

And the one he liked best of all – CAMULODUNUM. Colchester.

He spent hours saying the names over and over again, with just a hint of an Italian accent. He felt this was appropriate and brought out the best in the long, rounded words. Initially, he had been concerned that he might not be pronouncing them correctly. But no one really knew for certain how the Romans spoke their Latin. His guess was as good as anyone's. So that's what he did – he guessed, trying them out in different ways until he felt comfortable with them.

Sometimes he would put the names together and say them as if they were sentences. It felt like real Latin. LONDINIUM ISCA DUMNONIORUM. CAMULODUNUM VENTA

BELGARUM. . . .

Teacher after teacher had tried, of course, to stop Simon talking in class. Each would begin by believing that they would be the first to do so, but the most they ever achieved was a reduction in volume. The talking went on, a low, background noise, as untiring as the wind in the trees or the waves on the shore.

Simon's present teacher would occasionally interrupt the endless Latin litany by saying, "That's enough now, Simon." But he never sounded very hopeful.

It was a Youth Club trip to WILDWORLD, a big theme park with animals and rides. It was Saturday. Mr and Mrs Higgins, the Youth Club leaders, were taking a group of about twenty. Old Mr Wilkins, the Churchwarden, was helping too. They had travelled by minibus. They had queued to get their tickets and now they were inside, near the Adventure Playground which they were going to be allowed into later, last thing before going home. All the children were restless after the long trip and impatient to get started. Mrs Higgins was handing out printed sheets and Mr Higgins was trying to speak.

"Right everybody. Now listen carefully. I said listen. You lot at the back, you're not listening. This is important. We're going to start with the train ride. It's our turn to get on when the hooter goes off next, and – Julie Piper where do you think you're going? Pay attention and don't start wandering off yet. Now, after the train you can go round the animals and after that we're going to meet back here for lunch and then go to the rides together."

Everyone cheered at that.

"We're going to trust you older ones to go round in your groups, but you must stay together, you *must* stay together. Does everyone understand?

There were a few murmurs of, "Yes, Mr Higgins".

"Right, now, if you look at your timetables," he continued, "there's something I want to point out. . . ."

"Yes, yes, yes," said Simon, leaning over the back of Fraser's wheelchair and speaking into his left ear. "And they say *I* talk too much. We know all this. He went on and on about keeping in our groups and not talking to strangers while we were on the minibus. Why do we have to hear it all again? Why can't he just let us go and enjoy ourselves. No one stops grown-ups rabbiting, even when they've got nothing to say. At this rate it'll be time to go home before we've looked at anything," he broke off for just a moment to inhale deeply. "Mmm, can you smell those hot dogs? What do you say we go and get one as soon as we get off the. . . ."

"Simon! Are you listening?"

Simon stood up straight. "Yes, Mr Higgins."

"What was I saying, then?"

"Er. . . ."

But at that point the station hooter went off. Mr Higgins realised that there was no point in trying to prevent the tidal wave of children already surging towards the train. So he, his wife and old Mr Wilkins went with the flow, through the pretend ticket office, onto the miniature platform and aboard the tiny carriages. An attendant brought a ramp so that Fraser could wheel himself into a special compartment at the back,

where Simon, Mr Wilkins and a couple of the girls also sat.

The train took them at a gentle pace (rather too gentle as far as most of the children were concerned) right around the outside of the Park. When they returned to the station they were put in groups to go and look at the animals. They weren't allowed to choose their own groups and Simon ended up

with three older boys who were all friends. They weren't
unfriendly towards him, but they soon tired of his non-stop
chattering and gradually paid him less and less attention. As
they toured the enclosures, Simon began to lag behind and
feel left out.

When they were near the llamas, Simon caught a glimpse
of Fraser, amongst a crowd of people some distance away.
He told the other boys he was going to join Fraser's group.
They looked doubtful but didn't try to stop him as he went
off. But when Simon had struggled through the crowd to
reach the place where Fraser had been, by the snow leopard's
cage, there was no sign of him or the rest of his group. And
when he got back to the llamas, the three boys had also gone.

Oh well, he'd be all right on his own. He had a watch and
a copy of the timetable. He went round several more pens
and stopped at a large blue pool to see the sea-lions being
fed. After that it was a quarter to twelve. He checked the
timetable, it said to meet back by the Adventure Playground

at twelve thirty. Plenty of time yet. He looked around. Nearby
there was a large dome of fake rock. The entrance had been
made to look like a cave, above it was a sign which said
'Aquaworld'. That would be where all the aquariums were.
Great!

Simon spent forty very enjoyable minutes in the passages

of Aquaworld, and was pleased that he could identify most of the fish and other water creatures in the tanks. He knew them in English, but was delighted to find that the tank labels also gave their scientific names, in Latin. He stood by each of the tanks in turn and recited them aloud.

He left himself five minutes to walk back to the paved area by the Playground. He was feeling a bit guilty about leaving his group and was hoping to rejoin them again, unnoticed. He arrived back at exactly half past twelve and was surprised to find that he was the only one there. Surprised and a bit worried.

He double-checked the timetable. It definitely said twelve thirty, and this was the right place, wasn't it? Hadn't Mr Higgins said that they should meet back here? There was a map of WILDWORLD on the back of the sheet and there was only one Adventure Playground on it. There was another playground though, called the Kiddies' Playground. Perhaps that was where they were supposed to meet. Yes, that must be it.

The Kiddies' Playground was right over the other side of the Park. He was going to be late. He set off at a jog, stopping to look at the map and read the signposts at all the many footpath junctions along the way. The signposts bristled with arrows, radiating in all directions. Sometimes he started reading from the top and sometimes from the bottom, but 'Kiddies' Playground' always seemed to be on the very last arrow he read.

By the time he arrived it was twenty to one. There was no one there, at least, no one he knew.

It was now more than an hour since Simon had seen anyone from the Youth Club. He scanned the Park around him quickly, so quickly that his head began to spin. It must have been the other playground after all. But why hadn't they been there? What was that other important thing that Mr Higgins had told them? Something to do with the timetable. But what? It had been at that point that he'd started talking to Fraser. He gave a despairing groan and set off back the way he'd come, now running full tilt, bumping into people along the way, who turned to glare at him angrily.

When he got back and there was still no one, he slumped down on a bench. He would have to find someone in a WILDWORLD uniform and tell them what had happened. He would be taken to an information desk and his name would be announced over the loudspeakers. How embarrassing.

"Simon!"

Someone was calling. 'Simon' is quite a common name. It might not be him, but he hoped it was. He stood up and looked round.

"Simon! In here," the voice came from behind him. There, kneeling among the wood chippings of the Adventure Playground, was old Mr Wilkins. Simon ran through the gate. As he approached he saw that Mr Wilkins was kneeling beside a young girl who was lying, her leg twisted under her. She was sobbing and calling out for her Mum.

"She fell," explained Mr Wilkins.

"Shall I go for help?" asked Simon.

"No. Somebody already has. What you can do, though, is talk to her."

"Talk?"

"Yes. It'll help to take her mind off what's happened."

Simon looked down at the girl's tear-stained face, her eyes were staring, unfocused and frightened. Her sobbing was a

low constant whining, like the cry of a distressed puppy. She seemed quite unaware that they were beside her. "What shall I talk about?" he asked.

"Anything."

Simon got down on his hands and knees and racked his brains for something to say. He'd never had to do that before. He looked up again, helplessly. The old man smiled. "Anything will do. Just to keep her mind off the pain," he said.

So Simon turned back to her and made a start.

"Hello, my name's Simon," he stopped there, for once in his life hoping for a real conversation. But the girl didn't seem to have heard him.

"What's your name?" Still no reply.

"I'm here with our Youth Club." He stopped again.

"Tell her what you've seen today," prompted Mr Wilkins.

"We went on the train first of all. That was all right, but a bit slow. Then we got into our groups and went round to look at the animals. I . . . ," he glanced up at Mr Wilkins, "I sort of got separated from my group so I went round on my own. I watched the sea-lions being fed, they were really funny."

Simon saw that the girl had turned her face slightly and was now looking at him.

"But the best thing was Aquaworld. I spent ages in there 'cos I really like fish. I've got a tank of tropical fish at home.

I've got fourteen, five different sorts and they've all got names. My favourite is a clown loach (that's *Botia macracantha*). He's called Grumpy, 'cos his mouth goes down at the corners. Have you got any pets?"

The girl didn't respond, but she had stopped sobbing.

"After Aquaworld I came back to meet up with the rest of the Youth Club but they weren't here. It said on the timetable to meet by this playground at twelve thirty. But there must have been a change of plan. I've been running up and down ever since trying to find them. But now I've found Mr Wilkins, so I won't have to go and tell someone I'm lost. Serves me right really, I should have listened to Mr Higgins when he was talking to us at the start. I'll have missed most of the rides, I expect. Still, the animals were good. What do you like best, the animals or the rides?

The girl murmured something. Simon leant closer.

"Emma," she said. "My name's Emma."

Simon turned to Mr Wilkins triumphantly, "Her name's Emma."

Then the First Aid people arrived. They had a stretcher. Simon and Mr Wilkins stood back. Simon admired the way they handled the situation, the way they talked to Emma. He could learn a lot from them. They were friendly and reassuring. But she wouldn't answer when they asked her name, so Simon stepped forward to tell them.

"Well done, son," one of the men said, "Now we can get a message out. Looks like she's got separated from her family."

Emma cried out when they lifted her on to the stretcher but smiled faintly at Simon as they carried her away.

Mr Wilkins and Simon started walking to the rides to find the others. Mr Wilkins told Simon that he'd been watching him earlier, when Mr Higgins had been speaking, and guessed he hadn't heard about the change of plan. Everyone was supposed to meet back at twelve o'clock, instead of half past, to give them more time on the rides. So when Simon hadn't turned up, either with his own group or with Fraser's, at twelve, Mr Wilkins had said he'd wait for him. It must have been just as Simon was arriving that Mr Wilkins had seen the girl fall and gone to help her. Although the ground was covered in soft wood chippings it seems she landed awkwardly and may have broken her leg.

When Mr Wilkins had finished his explanation they carried on in silence.

"Aren't you going to tell me off?" Simon asked.

"What for?"

"Because I didn't listen. And I didn't stay with my group. And you had to wait for me."

"You've missed the rides. You know what you did wrong. What more can I say?"

"I talk too much. I know I talk too much," Simon confessed. But he'd known that for years. Simply knowing didn't help.

"On the other hand," Mr Wilkins continued, "talking to that little girl was good. If you hadn't been late, you wouldn't have been there to talk to her."

Simon didn't reply. This was new. This needed thinking about.

Mr Wilkins gave him a minute or so, before adding, "You've got a gift, Simon, the gift of the gab. Just remember that there is a time for silence and a time to speak."

Still Simon didn't reply. This all needed thinking about.

On the way home Simon sat next to Fraser on the minibus. He was so quiet that Fraser thought he must be feeling ill.

"Are you O.K.?" he asked.

"Yes, thank you," replied Simon. Then, slowly and deliberately, enjoying the words, as if he had just been granted the power of speech, Simon turned to Fraser and asked, "Have you had a good time today, Fraser?" And he didn't take his eyes off his friend, waiting for the reply.

Fraser was so astonished that he could only answer, "Yes, thank you, Simon."

Simon spent most of the journey back looking out of the window and wondering what this year's school report would say. He would be pleased if it were something along the lines of:

"Simon is learning that it can be to his advantage to pay close attention to instructions and he is trying hard to listen to others. He can bring comfort to those in distress with his natural cheerfulness."

Perhaps that was hoping for too much. The phrase that Mr Wilkins had used had stuck in his mind. He could see how true it was. But it's hard to change the way you are, even if you want to. It wouldn't happen overnight.

There was another saying, one he'd learned recently in school. It hadn't made much impression at the time. Now, though, he really felt he understood it. He nodded wisely and couldn't resist turning to Fraser to share the wisdom he had found. "You know, Fraser," he said, "there is a time for silence and a time to speak, but Rome wasn't built in a day."

"He's definitely not well," thought Fraser.

Sports Day

Belinda Baines hated Sports Day. She always had. Ever since that first one way back in the Infants.

On that occasion she was chosen to run in the Floppy Hat Relay. She was last to go for her team, the Yellows. They had been given the biggest, floppiest hat of all. When Helen Robson reached her and handed it over, Belinda had been jostled by the other waiting children and it got knocked over her eyes. She was so muddled she set off running in the wrong direction, still trying to get the hat on straight. She'd gone more than ten metres the wrong way down the track before she could see where she was going and turned round. Her team had been in the lead at the changeover, but now all the others were miles away, reaching the finishing line.

And when people saw what had happened they started to laugh. Everyone laughed. First the children and parents nearest the starting line because they were the first to see it, and then it spread in a wave down the course.

Belinda thought that she would never reach the end of that long and lonely track. When she finally did get there, hot and flustered and close to tears, everyone gave her a special clap and cheer. But it was too late. In her head the laughter sounded on.

Belinda was not really the sporty type anyway. Her parents and teachers were not quite sure what sort of type she was but it definitely wasn't sporty.

So when Sports Day came around next year and her teacher tried gently to encourage her to take part in at least one race, she wasn't surprised when Belinda quietly but firmly shook her head at each suggestion.

"What about the egg and spoon?" coaxed Miss Morton.

Belinda shook her head.

"The skipping race?"

Rope tangles up so easily. Belinda shook her head.

"The Floppy . . . No, perhaps not. What about the sack race, dear?" she said.

Belinda pictured herself somehow managing to get the sack over her head and blundering off into the crowd. She shook her head.

"Just a sprint, then?"

Belinda hesitated. A sprint. That was just running, wasn't it? What could go wrong with that? Something would. She shook her head.

"But Belinda, sweetheart," said Miss Morton lamely. "Sports Day is a Fun Day."

Belinda shook her head.

So she ended up being a Special Helper. From that year on it became accepted that Belinda Baines didn't actually take part. She was a Special Helper.

Only Mrs Craven disapproved. She was the deputy head and she was the strictest teacher in the school. She always wore dark clothes, dark blue or black, and was known as Craven the Raven. Even the other teachers were frightened of her. She was in charge of P.E. and at Sports Day she was always the race starter because she liked to make sure that everything ran on time. She also thought that children should be made to take part, whether they liked it or not. It was good for them.

Belinda helped Mrs Knight, she was in charge of all the equipment. Belinda ran up and down, bringing back the wooden eggs, spoons, skipping ropes, sacks, Wellington boots and Floppy Hats from the finish to the start so that they could be used again. She probably ran ten times as far as any of the competitors and although she wasn't really sporty, she enjoyed it.

Sometimes some of the other children got into a tangle with equipment or got confused about what they were supposed to do. When that happened she never laughed but looked on sympathetically, remembering what it felt like. She wasn't sorry she wasn't in any of the races, except. . . .

Except that after the novelty races, when she had brought everything back to the start, she would sit down, try on a hat or tie herself up with a rope and watch the sprints. Nothing ever did seem to go wrong. And she would begin to wonder if it might not be quite fun to have a go, to have all of the other children in your team cheering you on.

She supposed that she didn't really belong to any team now. But she still always hoped that Yellows would win, though they never did.

And then, when she was in Year 5 and Sports Day had come round again and she had finished fetching back all the equipment, had tried on a nice pair of red Wellingtons and was settling down on a comfy seat of folded sacks to watch the sprints, she saw Mrs Knight, who was her class teacher that year, leave the rest of their class and run over, clutching her clipboard.

"Belinda," she panted, "Helen's supposed to be in the sprint but she feels sick. There's a chance that Yellows might win this year, but only if someone from our class runs for them. I know you don't like. . . . "

"I'll do it," interrupted Belinda, "When am I on?"

"Now."

Belinda looked up and saw that Mrs Craven, in her navy blue tracksuit, was already bringing the starting whistle to her lips, her eyes on her watch. The nearest lane, the Yellow lane, was empty. Belinda knew that even if the Raven caught sight of her she wouldn't wait. Only as she stood up did she realise that she was still wearing the red Wellingtons. They were several sizes too big for her. But the whistle sounded as she stumbled to the start line and she set off anyway.

After just two strides she tripped and did a forward roll, really quite the best one she had ever done. The speed of it carried her straight back up onto her feet. The people nearby gasped when she tumbled but clapped when she stood again, so neatly. Then they noticed the boots and the laughter began.

But somehow the success of the forward roll inspired her. So, they were laughing again. Let them laugh. In fact, she'd make them laugh.

When the crowd clapped her recovery she made a little bow to them. When she saw them pointing and staring at her boots, she turned out her feet and walked Charlie Chaplin-style for the next ten metres. The laughter was building. But now it wasn't hurting her, crushing her, it was lifting her up, spurring her on. The other children had already finished the race, but no one was paying them any attention. Belinda brought up her hand to shield her eyes and stared after them.

She pretended to be horrified that they were so far ahead and stood on one leg, with the other raised sideways, bent at the knee, winding up her arms, like a cartoon character preparing to run. She hadn't known before that she knew how to do it, but she did and it set the Infants howling. She shot off again only to go flat on her face and beat the ground with her fists in mock frustration.

Then she got up as if the boots were made of lead. She kept them planted flat on the ground and swayed around, as if the weight of them made overbalancing impossible.

She mimed spitting onto her hands, clamped them around her legs and lifted each in turn, swinging them round in front of her, making her face a picture of pain and effort.

For the last ten metres she lay down and dragged herself slowly along with her hands and arms, legs trailing uselessly behind. When almost at the finish she raised herself up and stretched out a trembling hand for the line, only to collapse at the very last moment. She played dead for a few seconds then leaped to her feet, kicked off the wellies and crossed the line with a slow motion, exaggerated run, pushing her knees right up and pumping her arms back and forth, like that exercise of which Mrs Craven was so fond. Then she stopped and turned round, waving her arms above her head. The noise was deafening by now; laughing, clapping, cheering and whistling. A parent ran over and slapped a fourth place sticker on Belinda's tee-shirt. This she proudly displayed to the

crowd, before she was ushered over to the scorers to have her one point added to Yellows' total.

It wasn't enough for Yellows to win the trophy, which went to Blues, as usual. But the next day no one was talking about Blues' victory. The only topic of conversation in the playground and the Staffroom was Belinda Baines' Red Welly Sprint.

Mrs Craven made it clear that she was not the least bit impressed by Belinda's antics. But the other teachers could

101

see that even if Sport wasn't really Belinda's scene, she knew a thing or two about acting.

She took the starring rôle in the Christmas play that year. Not a comedy rôle, this time. She played a homeless child in Victorian London and there wasn't a dry eye in the house.

Everyone's looking forward to next Sports Day, though Mrs Craven seems to have changed her mind and now thinks that Belinda Baines should be banned.

For her own part, Belinda insists that she will be helping as usual and will only run if Yellows have another last minute emergency.

The little ones spend whole break times begging her to do the Red Welly Sprint again this year. But she shakes her head and says that it wouldn't be so funny the second time around. You should always leave your audience wanting more.

CD

It was CD who got me thinking. She was only with us for a few weeks but I'll never forget her.

Her full name is Columbine Dittander Nevsky. Her mother is English and her father Russian. But everyone called her CD, even the teachers.

She is proud of her Russian surname but her first names cause her great sorrow. I don't think they're that bad. At least they're interesting and unusual. (Unlike my first name, which is John. No middle name, just John.) But she hates them. They're both flower names. I looked them up in this book we've got at home.

Whenever she met new people she would introduce herself by giving her full name, slowly and clearly, "Columbine Dittander Nevsky". Then, after a short pause, "Were your parents kinder to you?"

This did seem to be the only thing that upset her, though. She only ever looked sad when she had just met new people.

Afterwards she would go on to say, "But please call me 'CD', I'd really like that." And everybody did. No one would upset CD if they could possibly help it.

There's a saying that's always bothered me. It's a saying grown-ups use quite a lot, especially teachers. They say: "Everyone is good at something".

I can understand why they say it and why they want it to be true. But it seems to me to be so *un*true. As far as I can see, some people are good at everything, some people are good at some things and some people are just plain useless.

Guess which category I come into.

There's this boy in our class called Philip and he's brilliant.

He's brilliant at maths. He's so far ahead of the rest of us that he has to work from special books.

He's brilliant at English. It's always one of his poems that gets read to the class as an example of how to write well. He knows all about the different sorts of words and rules for what you can and can't say.

He calls people peasants when they get things wrong. He says that Craig Sharpe is a peasant because he doesn't use past particles, whatever they are. And he points out to the teacher spelling mistakes she's made on the board.

He's brilliant at science. Whenever we do an experiment, he's already done it at home with his chemistry set or his microscope or equipment he made himself from yogurt pots and old coathangers.

At this point you might be saying to yourself, "So, he's good at that sort of thing, but what about art, music and sport? Is he any good at those?"

And the answers are: Yes, Yes and Yes.

His paintings and drawings are always on display. Last year he won a national design competition and there was an article about him in the paper. He's got grade six on the flute, grade four on the piano and a singing voice that makes the audience go "Ooh" at the Christmas Concert.

He is captain of the School football team, star of the local swimming club, holds the School record for the hundred metres sprint and has never been known to miss the ball when batting in rounders.

And is he ugly this boy? Are all his talents some kind of compensation for looking like Frankenstein's Monster on an off day? What do you think? All the girls fancy him. He got seventeen valentines last year. I've even heard my Mum say, "That one'll break a few hearts when he's older."

There is nothing that Philip cannot do. He is the bright star of the class and the rest of us are like dull planets. And I am the dullest of them all. Believe me, I'm not just being modest.

I have seen the tired look that teachers try to hide when they're explaining to me for the umpteenth time an idea that Philip already understood when he was being trundled round in his pushchair by his adoring mother.

I've seen another look – when a teacher first catches sight of one of my paintings.

And, although they don't think I do, I know why I'm always given the job of turning the pages for the recorders when the rest of the class is singing.

I've only ever played football for the School team once, and I'm sure that was just because Mr MacKenzie felt sorry for me. I tried to warn him that it was a mistake but he wouldn't listen. I scored an own goal. It happened like this.

There was this mass of arms and legs slogging it out in front of our goalmouth. It seemed like all the other players on the pitch were in there, fighting for the ball. Except me. I was standing to one side letting them get on with it. But then the ball trickled out and none of them noticed. It trickled out and stopped at my feet.

It was the first time I'd been anywhere near the ball since we started. And there was this open goal in front of me. It just seemed like too good an opportunity to miss. So I took a step back and whacked it. The ball lifted off the ground beautifully and soared between the posts.

I was jumping up and down and punching my fists in the air and wondering why it had all gone quiet when Philip walked over to me. Then I realised what I'd done. He didn't say a word. He just looked at me with that smile he has. That nasty smile. At half time I begged Mr MacKenzie to take me off and he had mercy upon me.

The teachers try to be kind, but the best they can come up with is comments like, "John is a cheerful boy. He is always friendly and helpful. He always tries his best."

Is that supposed to make me feel as good as Philip must feel? Who are they kidding? Philip is the bright star and I am the dullest planet. I am the Neptune of the class . . . or is it Pluto? You see, I told you I was hopeless. We only finished Space last week and I've already forgotten which planet goes where.

I'm telling you all this because it used to bother me a lot. Until CD arrived. Up till then Philip had been the one and only star in our Universe. There was no one even close to him. Then, for a few weeks, CD came into our lives. Even more dazzling. Let's say she was a comet – a dazzling comet. Yes, that sounds good.

Her Dad is a Russian writer and they were on a visit to England. They tour round a lot. She's lived everywhere: America, Brazil, France, Africa. Everywhere. Apart from English she can speak Russian and French. And she is brilliant. At everything. Like Philip.

Except that she's nice.

Suddenly my whole world changed. For years I'd been wishing I was Philip. And then suddenly I saw what a mistake I'd made.

CD was the same age as us but somehow much older. She didn't look down on us. She didn't use her cleverness to make us feel small. She didn't use nasty smiles. She didn't talk much about herself. She didn't want to be the centre of attention. She never went on about all the places she'd been to and how she could speak three languages. When she talked to you she sounded interested in what you had to say, made *you* feel important.

When CD arrived I was sure she'd soon get to be friends with Philip. Philip tried not to show it but it was obvious that he wanted to impress her. As well as pointing out spelling mistakes he was now telling our teacher when she'd put the commas in the wrong place. During a class discussion on Polar Bears he announced that he'd passed another music exam, with the highest possible grade. He got extinction, apparently. His poems became even longer and more depressing.

But despite all this CD didn't take much notice and Philip seemed to lose something of his brightness. More and more now in class the teacher would turn to CD and ask her opinion. She never pushed herself, the teacher would have to ask her directly, but she always had something interesting to say. She'd actually met some people you hear about in the news and been in important places when important things were happening. She spoke quietly but clearly. The rest of us sat spellbound. Except Philip. He would get a bit fidgety.

Then, the first time CD came swimming with us, when we were returning to School on the bus from the Leisure Centre, I took my usual position near the front. Most of the others were jostling for places at the back. The middle of the back seat was Philip's place and the seats close to him were highly valued. CD was last on. Philip had kept free the seat next to him. When CD climbed up the steps everyone watched. She looked right down the aisle, began to walk along it then swung round and sat next to me. The teacher got up to count heads and we were off.

"There's a place down the back for you, if you like," I said, thinking perhaps she hadn't seen it.

"Yes," she said. "I'd rather sit next to you though, if you don't mind."

"Sure," I replied.

Then she said, "We're having a party on Saturday, I was wondering if you'd like to come."

"Me? Why?" Straight away I wished I hadn't said that, it sounded so rude, but I was taken off guard.

She laughed. "Because I'd like it if you could."

"Is it your birthday?" I asked.

"No. It's the anniversary of the death of Pushkin. He was a Russian writer. I know it's weird, but that's the kind of thing my family celebrates."

"No. No, it's not weird," I said, trying to make up for earlier. Though I must admit, it did sound a funny reason for having a party.

"Are you going to ask Philip?" I couldn't stop myself asking.

"I don't think so," she said.

She seemed to know how surprised I was feeling, about her invitation. "A lot of people like you, you know," she said after a while.

Another shock.

"They do? Who?"

"People in the class. And the teachers. They like you a lot."

"How can you tell?"

"Oh, the way they talk to you. The way they look at you."

"Really?"

"Yes."

This was wonderful. I'd never felt this good in my whole life before. But was it true? Perhaps CD was just being nice. I thought of all the mistakes I made. How could it be true?

"Except when I get everything wrong. Which is all the time," I muttered, turning away and looking out of the window.

"Well, you may not be the cleverest person in the world. And that's bound to be trying even for the most patient teacher. But they still like you. And that's what matters."

"Is it?"

"Yes."

Again, I just had to ask, "Do you think the teachers like Philip?"

"You know," she said, "you really shouldn't worry so much about Philip."

So I went to the party, with a couple of others from the class. Not Philip. It wasn't like any other party I've been to. There was tons of food and drink. Things I'd never tasted before. That's all we did. We sat round this huge table that took up most of their flat and we ate and drank and talked. Like a grown-up party. It sounds boring, but it wasn't. Mr and Mrs Nevsky are just as nice as CD. Sometimes I'm shy, but I wasn't then. I think I did more talking than eating. That's rare for me.

At the end, just before we went home, Mr Nevsky pulled out a book from one of the piles on the floor (there were books everywhere, far too many for the shelves) and he read a poem by this writer, Pushkin. It was in Russian, so of course I didn't understand a word. But that didn't matter. The way he read it was like listening to music. The words didn't matter, just the sound his voice made, almost singing.

When I got home I tried to tell Mum and Dad about the party, but I couldn't explain it properly. I just made the whole thing sound strange. Perhaps it was. But it was still the best party I've ever been to.

Not long after that, CD had to leave. We were all devastated. Me especially, as you can imagine. In assembly on her last day Mrs Fuller, our headteacher, said that CD wished to say a few words. She got up from our row and walked to the front, she was carrying a book.

In her quiet, clear voice she said how much she had enjoyed being with us and how she would miss us all.

"Yesterday," she continued, "my Dad had to go to the bookshop in town. I asked him to get a book which we could give to the School. I should have known it was a mistake, he's never been good at presents. He chose some Russian poetry. I suppose we must just be thankful it's an English translation.

"We've written our names on the front," she continued, holding up the book so that everyone could see. "It should be done inside the cover but, as Mum pointed out, not many people are ever likely to look inside. Anyway, we hope you won't forget us completely.

"I'd like John King to accept it on behalf of the School," she said.

So I got up and went to the front. We shook hands, formally.

"Sorry it's not something more interesting," she said as she gave me the book.

"It's the thought that counts," I replied.

She considered these words and nodded slowly, as if she had never heard the saying before, as if I had just invented it. Funnily enough, right then I felt as if I had.

I looked at the three signatures on the front, and the title.
"It's Pushkin," I said. "He's my favourite author."
She laughed. She thought I was joking. But I wasn't.
Everyone clapped and all the teachers were beaming.
Beaming at CD and, yes, beaming at me too.